STRANGE RELATIONS

Nik heard the whistle, a piping call that was like a throb of pain beginning in his head and running along his nerves to make his flesh tingle. Three times that shattering call came.

The bushes shook, spilling the lurkers into sight. They came scuttling, at first on hands and knees. Then, from a crouch, they launched themselves at him.

Nik had expected animals, but these—these were men!

Also by Andre Norton
Published by Ballantine Books:

THE BEAST MASTER

CATSEYE

DARK PIPER

DREAD COMPANION

GRYPHON IN GLORY

THE JARGOON PARD

LORD OF THUNDER

POSTMARKED THE STARS

STAR GATE

STAR GUARD

VICTORY ON JANUS

'WARE HAWK

THE X-FACTOR

NIGHT OF MASKS

A Del Rey Book

BALLANTINE BOOKS • NEW YORK

*The author wishes to express appreciation
to Charles F. Kelly, who supplied the information
leading to the development of Dis.*

NIGHT OF MASKS

1

Outside, the day was as gray as the wall behind Nik Kolherne, where he hunched under the arch of roof well above his head. The steady drizzle of rain was as depressing as those thoughts he could not push out of his mind, even by the most determined effort. His thin-fingered hands moved restlessly, smoothing the front of the worn and colorless jump coat that hung in folds about his thin chest and shoulders. The damp had him shivering, but he made no move to seek shelter through the door immediately behind him.

There was shelter inside but nothing else in the big barracks of the Dipple. Those without family ties held no more rights than the tentative possession of a bunk, and that only as long as they could defend it, should one of their fellows in misfortune take a liking to it.

Nik's right hand came up in a gesture now so much a part of him that he was no longer aware when he made it. Without actually touching his face, his palm covered chin and nose, masking all that lay below his large, penetratingly brilliant blue-green eyes. He hugged the wall of the entranceway, giving good room to two men splashing in from the yard. Neither noticed him as they pushed into the barracks.

Moke Varn and Brin Peake. In the world of the Dipple, they were solid citizens of a sort. Or should one correct that? Nik, his hand mask still upheld, searched for a proper term to cover the activities and standing of Moke Varn and Brin Peake.

Maybe not solid citizens in the sense used by the free

world beyond the Dipple gates. But at least they had power, and their standing within these walls was firmly based. And since it was undoubtedly true that the Dipple would continue to be Nik's complete world, its terms of reference must be the ones used in evaluating his fellow unfortunates—not that either Moke or Brin considered himself unfortunate.

Once there had been no Dipple; once there had been no war. Once—once a little boy had been someone different, very different. His blue-green eyes held a shadow as Nik stared dully into the slanting lines of rain. But there *had* been the war, and all the dispossessed flotsam had been swept up and thrown into the refuse heaps of the Dipples on many planets—to rot forgotten, as if they were not people at all but statistics and footnotes in some little-read history book of a time the free worlds were now working hard to forget. The war had ended in an exhausted tie, but hate lingered, smoldering under the surface of the here and now, a hate that—

This time Nik's fingers closed tight against his face. His stomach heaved in a retching spasm. The furrows of scarred skin were harsh under his touch. He had a mask all right, one out of nightmares and one he could never put aside. Ten years ago a freighter spacer had been temporarily turned into an escape ship for a small colony on a frontier world lying within enemy-patrolled territory. That freighter had been pursued by the enemy and had crashed on a barren moon.

How in the name of the Spirit had Nik survived that disaster anyway? Why had a child with a torn and burned face continued to live when all those about him had mercifully died? Then—out of nowhere—had come rescue, men in space armor tramping into the small area of the ship where Nik had cowered almost witless. After their coming, there was a jumble of impressions cloaked with delirium and pain, the terror of the unknown. Finally, there had been the hospital here at the Dipple on Korwar. Then—just the Dipple in which he was always alone.

He dreamed—yes, sometimes he dreamed of a country under another sky with a different tint and a warmer sun. But was that a real memory or just a dream? He could remember only such small bits after the crash. His sole link with that other world was the identity disk they had found on him—Nik Kolherne, a name combined with symbols that had not made sense to any authority here. At first, he had asked questions of his fellow internees until their reactions to his gargoyle face had driven him into a solitary life and to the reading tapes.

To a tape, it did not matter that Nik was only human-seeming from eye level to the top of his head with its tight curls of wiry hair the color of burnished jet. So he had fled into the world of the mind, soaking up materials upon which his imagination fed, so that he *was* able to lead another life—one he could summon up at need, perhaps as vivid as that a haluce drinker knew.

Sometimes nowadays Nik was more aware of that other life than he was of the Dipple, though a ripple of disquiet came like a half-heard warning now and then to disturb his dreaming. But he pressed that down, strove to rout it utterly. He had his dream world, and in it he was free! He clung to it passionately.

The need to return to his fantasy now drove him forth into the rain, and he scuttled from the barracks to the next building, the supply warehouse. The bored guard at the door did not see Nik flit by—he was an expert at finding hiding places. Seconds later he reached his latest one, a tiny opening through which he could squeeze, to wriggle up on some crates and lie on a ragged bit of blanket.

Nik stretched out. The layer of stuff beneath his sharp shoulder blades was not thick, but he was oblivious to the discomfort. The drum of rain on the roof not too far above him was soothing, and he closed his eyes, ready to plunge into his dream.

"—has to be right—all a one-time blast-off—"

Those words had no part in the fantasy Nik was

creating. In themselves, they were only a minor disturbance, but something in the voice brought Nik's eyes open, made him listen.

"No move until we are sure—"

"And while we're sittin' on our fins waitin' for a take-off, the whole deal can turn sour—into a real bad burn-off—"

Nik hitched around on his pad and began a worm's progress to the end of the box from which he should be able to view the speakers. There was no light in the gloom below. The meeting had all the aspects of a private one. Of course, there were a good many undercurrents in the Dipple. This was not the first time Nik had been on the fringe of secrets or learned what could prove dangerous should his knowledge be discovered by others.

"I repeat—in this there can be *no* chances—not in the groundwork. It's too big to allow any off-course work. Do you understand that?"

Stowar! Nik could see the two figures below only as shadows among other shadows, but that one voice he knew. Stowar was big here in the Dipple—a king shark to such small predators as Moke and Brin. If a man could raise the price to buy into the Thieves' Guild and so open a door out of this rat hole, Stowar was the negotiator who carried out the deal. Stowar had things to sell, too—haluce and other drugs. He had contacts, they said clear up the Veeps of the half world on Korwar and even off-world, too.

Nik shivered. To eavesdrop on one of Stowar's little deals could be very dangerous. He dug his nails into the surface of the box on which he lay and tried to still his breathing, not daring to withdraw for fear they could hear his movements.

"All right—so no chances." The other sounded impatient and not a bit overawed by Stowar. "But that course's been plotted twice—an' each time it cost us a fistful. If we have to go to Margan again, he'll up the price on us. He's no fool, and he'll do a little thinking on his own."

"There are ways of dealing with Margan—"

"Yeah, and those wouldn't be healthy either. Meddle with Margan and you'll have the Brethren down with blasters out, ready to do some cookin'! Don't you planet crawlers ever forget that Margan is our man, and we'll cut in for him. We *need* Margan; he's the best course man in the business. This trick of yours is just one trip as far as the Brethren see it."

The Brethren! Nik's mind was wholly freed of the mist of fantasy now. Stowar could well have contacts with the Brethren—the space-borne section of the Thieves' Guild who sought their prey on loosely held frontier worlds. That meant this deal could be very big. Though Stowar might head the lawless element in the Dipple, to the Guild itself he was a small operator to whom the real Veeps threw the small crumbs.

"Commendable comment. But our friend here is right on one point. This is no time to come in for a two-fin landing, Bouvay—"

A third man down there! Nik tried to pick out his shadow, but he must be standing, out of sight, in the crack between the crate on which Nik himself perched and its fellow.

Stowar had been easy for Nik to identify because, seemingly indifferent to Nik's disfigurement, he had, from time to time, given the boy small tasks, Nik's only means of earning a credit or two to finance the purchase of new tapes.

"All right. But a third run with Margan will be suspicious—maybe make real trouble."

"We are duly warned," agreed the unknown in the crack. "You say we have five more days?"

"Five more days for this course. Then you wait three planet months before you can try again."

"So be it. We'll just have to wait it out."

"But—" Stowar began an instant protest.

"Five days—to find our man, to set up the whole plan? It can't be done. I've tried some so-called impossible things in my time, orbited in on one or two of them, too. But short of going into stass and taking all

13

of Korwar with us, we're going to have to pass on this run and wait out those three months."

"And in the meantime"—Stowar's voice soared—"we can see i'Inad made some change to spoil everything. I say—much better make it a straight snatch—"

"Which is completely impossible," came a chill retort. "They have the ultimate in security. The pattern can't be broken by us except by the setup Heriharz has worked out. You yourself were urging caution just a moment ago, friend."

"Caution, reasonable caution, certainly. But every delay gives i'Inad a chance to counter us—"

There was a soft laugh from the dark alley. "Seems an impasse, doesn't it? But I have faith in the stars, Stowar. We'll either turn up our key or—"

"Or have to write it all off. Some tricks you can't pull ever. This is a dead rocket if I ever saw one."

"Your commander doesn't agree with you, Bouvay, but it's your privilege to cry off if you want."

Only a mutter replied to that. Nik tensed. That voice out of the dark carried a note of confidence rarely heard here. The diction was smooth, the tone authoritative. This was no Dipple dweller. Everyone knew that the Guild had their undercover men in the Planet Guard, among the port authorities, with the spacer crews. This man could well be one of them.

"Three months—" That was Stowar, but this time there was a resigned note in his voice. "And at the end of three months—if we have not found the right man?"

"Then we make some other decision. But FC says we will."

Some one of his listeners snorted. "Then why'n green blazes don't that tame machine tell us *where* to find him? Maybe he ain't on Korwar. Ever think of that?"

"The probabilities, according to FC, are that he is. Look about you, man—what's in a Dipple?"

"A bunch of dim beats as has had it!" returned Bouvay promptly.

"According to your estimation, yes. But on the other hand, right between these walls we have a big cross section of galactic races and types. When they swept up refugees and deportees and dropped them down here, there wasn't any sorting. We have inhabitants from forty worlds, survivors of ship disasters, a mixture such as you won't find anyplace else."

"Except in another Dipple," cut in Stowar.

"Just so. And where is the nearest other Dipple? On Kali, a good six-month flight from here. How long have we been sifting the stock right in front of us? About one month. FC says the probabilities are he *is* here; we just have to find him. And because you haven't turned up the proper combination yet, Stowar, is no reason that such a person does not exist."

"I know." The Dipple man sounded more confident. "You're right. If there's such a man, we ought to have him here. There's a mix as will turn up about anything. The only thing they've in common is that they all look human."

"That's the only factor he has to have," commented the unknown. "Our man *has* to register human or he can't get by the spy line. So, we practice patience and—"

Nik was startled. The speaker had stopped, almost in mid word. All Nik caught thereafter was a sharp hiss. The shadows that were Stowar and Bouvay had frozen. Nik listened. His mouth was dry, his heart beginning to sharpen its beat. Somehow he could sense a wariness, an alerting. Had they discovered him? But how could they—?

He cried out, tried to jerk free, kicking out with one foot, but the hold on his right ankle remained firm. It was as if his whole right leg was glued to the top of the crate. Then the power in the left suddenly failed. That leg lay beside the right, both now immovable. Thoroughly frightened, Nik tried to lever his half-dead body up by using his arms, only to have them fail him in turn. He was pinned to the surface under him as if he had never had any power to move.

Then he did move, but not by his own will. Stiff in his invisible bonds, his whole body rose from the crate and

15

slid out over the open space where the men he had spied upon stood waiting for him. Shaking with a fear he could only control to the point of not screaming his terror aloud, Nik sank down, helpless to defend himself against any action they chose to take.

"Stack rat!"

Nik was still descending when that fist snapped out of the general gloom and connected against his cheekbone with force enough to scramble his senses. He was aware dazedly of another blow. And then there was only darkness until light beat into him, and he tried to raise his hands to shield his eyes, blinded by the full glare of a torch.

"—you're away off orbit—"

"I don't think so. Look, man; just use your eyes for once!"

A painful grip on Nik's hair jerked his head closer to the light. He closed his eyes.

"Who is he, Stowar?"

"Just what Bouvay called him—a stack rat. Gives most of the people horrors, so he keeps out of sight."

"Sure—look at his face! Enough to turn your insides straight out of you! What do you mean about his being any good to us? Give him a blast and let it go at that. Put him outta his misery. He can't enjoy life lookin' like that."

"His face—" The voice from behind the torch sounded speculative. "That doesn't matter too much. What is important is that he's about the right size and age—or looks it anyway. It's just possible we have what we want. If he goes, there'll be no one to ask questions—he won't be missed."

"I don't believe you can use *him!*" Bouvay was emphatic.

"You don't have to. But I believe in luck, Bouvay, and it may be that Lady Luck is pushing comets across the board to us right now! Gyna can do wonders with raw material."

"Anyway, we'll have to do something with him."

16

That was Stowar once more. "Stow him in the box there, and I'll send a couple of the boys to take him to my place. How long does this tie of yours last?"

"Not much longer, unless I want to burn out the unit."

"Fair enough. I'll just take care of that problem."

The last words Nik heard were those from Bouvay. For the second time he was struck and sagged back into the dark from which the torchlight had momentarily dragged him.

He was lying on a hard surface—the blanket must have been dragged from under him on the crate. And this was the first time he had come out of a dream with a badly aching head. Dream? But this had not been one of his visits to his secret world at all! Nik found thinking a shaky process, and the feeling of nausea, which, oddly enough, seemed located more in his painful head than his middle, swooped down into the proper section of his anatomy as he tried to move.

The patchwork of recent memories began to fit into a real pattern. He lay with closed eyes and forced himself to make those memories whole. The warehouse—and the three who met there—Stowar! Nik's suddenly tensing muscles hurt. He had been caught listening to some private plan of Stowar's!

Now he tried to make his ears serve to inform him on his present surroundings. He was lying on a hard surface—that much he already knew—but before he opened his eyes and so perhaps gave away his return to consciousness, he wanted to learn everything else he could.

There was a sound—a murmur that might be the rise and fall of voices from a distance. Now that he had himself in hand, Nik could use his nose, too. The faintly sweet smell—that was only one thing, Canbia wine. Just one inhabitant of the Dipple could afford Canbia—Stowar—so he was now in Stowar's quarters.

Nik dared to open his eyes and looked up into complete darkness. With great effort, he lifted a limp hand. A fraction of an inch from his side, it struck against a

17

solid surface. The left hand discovered a similar obstruction on the other side.

He could see light now—a faint outline over him, enough to tell him he was in a box. In a moment of raw panic, he struggled to sit up, only to discover the effort beyond his powers. Then all the patience and self-control he had so painfully learned went into action. So—he was in a box. But he was still alive, and if they had wanted to erase him, they would not have gone to the trouble of carting him here. Stowar wanted no trouble in his own quarters.

Nik puzzled over his fragmentary memories of those last moments when he had been so strangely lifted out of hiding and delivered, helpless, into the hands of the enemy. The method of attack did not concern him now; the reason for his being here did. What had the stranger said—that he was the right age and size and that his face was not important. Not important.

The sound of boot heels on the floor outside his prison made Nik strive once more to move. His hands—he could pull them up a little. The rest of him seemed frozen still.

Then the cover over him banged back, and he was looking up into the face of a stranger. The skin was browned in the deep coloring of a spaceman, so that the single topknot of hair above the almost totally shaven skull looked like a white plume in contrasting fairness. The regular features were handsome, though the eyes were so heavily droop-lidded that Nik had no idea of their coloring.

And now there was a quirk of a smile about the stranger's lips, giving a certain relaxation to his expression. Nik found himself losing the first sharp edge of his apprehension.

A bronze hand swooped down and caught at the front of Nik's jacket. He was drawn up in that hold as if his own weight were feather-light as far as the other was concerned. Then an arm about his shoulders steadied him on his feet, and he was standing.

"Don't worry. You'll be able to blast in a minute."

Under the stranger's guidance, Nik regained enough power to step out of the box and take a stumbling step or two. He was lowered onto a stool, his back against the wall of the room. The other sat down, facing him.

The stranger wore space leather and ship boots. The triple star of a captain winked from the throat latch of his tunic. He leaned forward, his fists on his knees, to survey Nik. For the first time in years, Nik Kolherne made no attempt to mask his ruined face with his hand. There was a kind of defiance in his desire for the other to see every scar.

"I was right!" The white-hair plume rippled as the stranger nodded briskly. "You *are* our probability."

2

Nik's head and shoulders were propped against the wall, and as the stranger leaned forward, their eyes were much on a level. He matched the searching stare. And now he said, "I don't know what you mean."

"Not needful that you do—yet. How long have you had that face?"

"Ten years, more or less. I was fished out of a wreck during the war."

"Nobody tried to patch it up for you?"

Nik willed his hand to remain on his knee, willed himself to face that frank appraisal without an outward tremor. There was no disgust, no shrinking, only real bewilderment in the other's expression. And seeing that, Nik replied with the truth.

"Why didn't they fix my face? Well, they tried. But it seemed I couldn't adapt to growth flesh—it sloughed off after some months. And other experiments, they cost too much. No one had the credits to spend on Dipple trash."

That had been the worst of his burden in the years behind him, knowing that right here in Korwar were cosmetic surgeons who might have been able to give him a human face again. Yet the costly experimentation needed by a patient who could not provide natural rooting for growth flesh was far out of his reach.

"Something could be done even now."

Nik refused to rise to the bait. "I'm not the son of a First Circle family," he replied evenly. "And if growth flesh fails, there's little they can do, anyway."

20

"Don't be so sure." The stranger got to his feet. "Don't discount luck."

"Luck?" queried Nik.

"Yes, luck! Listen, boy. I'm on a winning streak now. The comets are all hitting stars on my table! And you're a part of it. What would you do for a new face—the face you should have had?"

Nik's stare was set. Plainly this was meant in all seriousness. Well, what would he give, do, for a face—a real face again? He didn't have to hesitate over that answer.

"Anything!" It would be worth it, any pain or sacrifice on his part, any effort, no matter how severe or prolonged.

"All right. We'll see. Stowar—!" At the space officer's call, the Dipple man came to the door of the room. "I'm standing for Kolherne."

Stowar's flat, emotionless eyes slid over the boy. He was frowning a little. "The choice is yours—now," he returned, but not as if he agreed. "When do you take him, Leeds?"

"Right away. Now, Kolherne"—the other swung to face Nik once more—"it's up to you. If you want that face, you have to be prepared to earn it, understand?"

Nik nodded. Sure he understood. Anything you wanted you had to earn, or take—if you were strong enough and well armed enough to make the grab practical. He did not doubt that Leeds was either one of the Guild or the Brethren, operating well on the cold side of any planetary or space law. But that did not bother him. Within the Dipple, one learned that the warmth of the law was for the free, not for the dispossessed and helpless. He was willing to walk the outlaw's road; that was no choice at all with the promised award ahead.

"This is the story—you're the son of a spaceman, my former first officer. I found you here, will sign bond for you. That will release you from the Dipple. The guard won't do much checking. They're glad to get anyone off the roster legally. Got anything you want to collect from a lock box, Nik?"

21

What did he have to call his own? A tape reader and a packet of tapes. Nothing he really needed. And those belonged to the Kolherne who had no hope at all—save through their temporary means of escape. Now something as wild as anger or fear was boiling inside Nik; he could hardly keep it bottled down. He did not recognize it as hope.

"No—" His voice seemed so little under his control that he did not say more than that one word.

"Then, let's go!" Again that strong grasp bringing him up to his feet, steadying him. He stumbled across the room, out into Stowar's business quarters, hardly noting Moke Varn there. Moke was of no importance any more. This was one of Nik's dreams taking on the solid reality of flesh in the hand guiding him ahead, in the surprised expression on Moke's flat face, in the bubbling and churning in Nik's middle. He was drunk with hope and the excitement Leeds had fired in him.

"Now pay attention." Leeds' tone sharpened as they emerged into a mist that had followed the rain. "My name is Strode Leeds. I'm master of the Free Trader Serpent. Got that?"

Nik nodded.

"Your father was my first officer in the Day Star when the war broke out. He was killed when we were jumped by the Afradies on Jigoku. I've been searching the Dipples for you for the past three years. Luck, O Luck, you are riding my fins today! I couldn't have set this up better if I'd known you were going to come down out of the roof back in that warehouse. You stick with me, boy, and that luck has just naturally got to rub off a little on you!"

Leeds was smiling, the wide satisfied smile of a gambler ready to scoop up from the table more than his hoped-for share of the counters.

Nik, still a little wobbly on his legs, tried to match his stride to the captain's, willing to go where Leeds wished, holding to him the promise the other had made, the promise that still seemed part of a dream. He listened to Leeds' glib explanation at the Dipple

Registration and nodded when the supervisor perfunctorily congratulated him on his luck. There it was—luck again. He who had never remembered seeing the fair face of fortune was beginning to believe in it with some of the fervor Leeds exhibited.

Then they were out of the Dipple. Nik dragged a little behind his companion, savoring that small wonder that was part of the larger. In all his existence on Korwar, he had been out of the Dipple's gray hush no more times than he could reckon on the fingers of one hand. Once to the hospital in a vain attempt to have them try skin growth on him again, to return defeated and aching with the pain of the medical verdict that it was useless. And the rest on hurried trips to the nearest tape shop to buy the third-hand, scratchy records that had been all the life he cared for. But now he was out—really out!

Leeds punched the code of a flitter at the nearest call box. It was beginning to rain again, and the captain jerked the shoulder hood of his tunic up over his head. Nik licked the moisture from that scar tissue that should have been lips. Even rain was different beyond the Dipple walls; it tasted sweet and clean here.

As they seated themselves in the cab and Leeds set the controls, he glanced at the boy. The captain was no longer smiling. There was a sharp set to his mouth and jaw.

"This is only the first step," he said. "Gyna and Iskhag, they have the final decision."

Nik snapped back into tense rigidity. One part of him was apprehensive. So—there was a flaw in this "luck" after all? This was only what all his life had led him to expect.

"But," Leeds was continuing, "since the main play is mine, I've the right to say who's going to lift into this orbit—"

Nik's first seething glow had faded; his old-time control was back. All right, so Leeds had talked him out of the Dipple. He'd have to go right back if the captain's plan failed. Nowhere on Korwar could he

23

show this face and hope for a chance for freedom—
unless it was freedom to starve.

Korwar was a pleasure planet. Its whole economy
was based on providing luxury and entertainment for
the great ones of half the galaxy. There was no place in
any of its establishments for Nik Kolherne. On another
world, he might have tried heavy labor. But here they
would not even accept him for the off-world labor draft
once they took a good look at him.

The flitter broke away from the traffic lanes of the
city and slanted out on a course that would take it to
the outer circle of villas and mansions. Nik gazed down
at a portion of the life he had never seen, the wealth of
vegetation culled from half a hundred different worlds
and re-rooted here in a mingled tapestry of growing
and glowing color to delight the eyes. They lifted over a
barrier of gray thorn, where the pointed branches and
twigs were beaded with crystalline droplets—or were
those flowers or leaflets? Then the craft came down on
the flat roof of a gray-green house, part of its structure
seeming to run back into the rise of a small hill behind
it.

The rain splashed about them and poured off in
runlets to vanish at the eaves of the building. Nik
followed Leeds out of the flier, saw it rise and return to
the city. Then he shivered and wiped his sleeve across
his face.

"Move!" That was Leeds, giving his charge little or
no time to look about him. The captain had his boots
planted on a square block in the roof. He reached out a
long arm and caught at Nik, pulling him close. There
was a shimmer about the edges of the block on which
they stood. Abruptly the rain ceased to drive against
them. Then the shimmer became solid, a silver wall,
and Nik was conscious of a whine that was half vibration.

The silver became a shimmer again, vanished. They
were no longer on the roof under the dull gray of the
sky but in a small alcove with a corridor running from
right to left before them.

24

"This way." Leeds' pace was faster; Nik stumbled in his wake.

The walls about them were sleekly smooth and the same cool gray-green as the outer part of the house. But Nik had the feeling that they were not in that structure but beneath it, somewhere in the soil and rock upon which it stood.

Just before the captain reached what appeared to be a solid wall at the end of the corridor, that surface rolled smoothly back to the left, allowing them to enter a room.

The carpet under Nik's worn shoepacs was springy, a dark red in color. He blinked, trying to take in the room and its inhabitants as quickly as possible, with all the wariness he could summon.

There were two eazi-rests, their adaptable contours providing seating for a man and a woman. Nik's hand flashed up to his face, and then he wondered. She must have seen him clearly; yet there was none of that distaste, the growing horror he had expected to see mirrored in her eyes. She had regarded him for a long moment as if he were no different from other men.

She was older than he had first judged, and she wore none of the fashionable gold or silver cheek leaf. Her hair was very fair and hung in a simple, unjeweled net bag. Nor did her robe have any of the highly decorative patterns now preferred. It was a blue-green, in contrast to the red cushions supporting her angular body, restful to the eye. Between the fingers of her right hand rested a flat plate of milky semiprecious stone, and from that she licked, with small, neat movements of her tongue, portions of pink paste, never ceasing to regard Nik the while.

In the other eazi-rest was a man whose ornate clothing was in direct contrast to the simplicity of the woman's. His gem-embroidered, full-sleeved shirt was open to the belt about his paunch, showing chest and belly skin of a bluish shade. His craggy features were as alien in their way to the ancestral Terran stock of the others as that blue-tinted skin. His face was narrow, seeming to ridge on the nose and chin line, with both those features oversized and jutting sharply. And there were two points of teeth showing against the darker blue of his lips even when his mouth was closed, points that glistened in the light with small jewel winks. His head was covered with a close-fitting metal helmet boasting whirled circles where human ears would be set.

There were non-Terran, even non-humanoid, intelligent species in the galaxy, and Korwar pulled many of their ruling castes into tasting its amusements, but Nik had never faced a true alien before.

Both woman and alien made no move to greet Leeds, nor did they speak for a long moment. Then the woman put down her plate and arose, coming straight across the room to stand facing Nik. She was as tall as he, and when suddenly her hand struck out, catching his wrist, she bore down his masking hand with a strength he could not have countered without an actual struggle.

Grave-eyed, she continued to study his wrecked face with a penetrating concentration as if he presented an absorbing problem that was not a matter of blood, bones, and flesh but something removed from the human factor entirely.

"Well?" Leeds spoke first.

"There are possibilities—" she replied.

"To what degree?" That was the alien. His voice was high-pitched, without noticeable tone changes, and it had an unpleasant grating quality as far as Nik was concerned.

"To the seventieth degree, perhaps more," the woman replied. "Wait—"

She left Nik and went to the table by the eazi-rests. She spun a black box around to face a blank wall. And the alien pressed a button on his seat so that it swung about to face the wall also. There was a click from the box, and a picture appeared on the blank surface.

A life-size figure stood there, real enough to step forward into the room—a man, a very young man, of Nik's height. But Nik's attention was for the unmarred, sun-browned face whose eyes were now level with his own. The features were regular. He was a good-looking boy; yet there was an oddly mature strength and determination in his expression, the set of his mouth, and the angle of jaw.

The woman had stepped to one side. Now she glanced from the tri-dee cast to Nik and back again.

"He says growth flesh did not take on transplant," Leeds commented.

"So? Well, there are ways—" Her reply was almost absent. "But look, Iskhag—the hair! Almost, Strode, I can believe in this luck fetish you swear by. That hair—"

Nik looked from those features to the hair above them. The wiry curls on the pictured head were as tight as his and just as black.

"It would seem," shrilled Iskhag, "that the FC was right. The probabilities of success at this point outweigh those of failure. If, Gyna, you think you have a chance of performing your own magic—?"

She shrugged and snapped off the tri-dee cast. "I will do what I can. The results I cannot insure. And—it may be only temporary if the growth fails again—"

"You know the newest techniques, Gentle Fem," Leeds interrupted, "and those are far more successful than the older methods. We can promise you unlimited resources for this." He looked to Iskhag, and the blue alien nodded.

"Does he understand?" The high chitter of Iskhag's speech came as he looked at Nik.

Leeds took out a small box and flipped a pellet he took from it into his mouth. "He understands we promise him a face again, but that it has to be earned. Also, I signed him out of the Dipple and will guarantee his Guild fee—"

The woman came back to Nik, her long skirt rustling across the carpet. "So you will earn your face, boy?"

Before he could avoid it, her hand made another of those quick moves, and her fingers closed on his misshapen chin, holding it firmly.

"You are entirely right," she continued as if the two of them were alone in the room. "Everything must be earned. Even those to whom birth gives much make payment in return, in one form or another. Yes, I shall strive to give you a face, for our price."

For the first time, Nik summoned up enough courage to take a part in this conversation about him and his affairs.

"What's the price?"

The woman loosened her hold on him. "Fair enough." She nodded as if that question had, in some obscure way, pleased her. "Tell him, Leeds." That was no request but an order.

"So"—Iskhag swung his eazi-rest back to its former position—"take him to his quarters, tell him—make all ready. We have been too long about this matter now!"

Leeds smiled. "In a matter of this kind, haste makes for mistakes. Do you wish for mistakes, Gentle Homo?"

"I wish for nothing but to set a good plan to work, Captain." Was there a shadow of withdrawal in Iskhag's reply?

The woman had picked up her plate of pink paste. Once more her tongue licked, in small, tip-touch movements, at its contents, but she watched Nik as Leeds caught him by the shoulder and gave him an encouraging shove toward the door.

Down the corridor, past the alcove where they had entered, then through a second sliding doorway they went, and they were in another luxurious room. Leeds motioned Nik to a seat on a wide divan.

"Hungry?" the captain asked. Without waiting for an answer, he went to a dial server on the wall and spun a combination. A table slid out, drawer fashion, the closed dishes on its surface numbering at least six. Nik watched as it moved into place before the divan, and Leeds sat down beside him to snap up the heat covers.

"Tuck in!" the captain urged, sampling the contents of the nearest dish himself.

Nik ate. The food was so different from the mess-hall fare of the Dipple that he could hardly believe it could be called by the same name. He did not know, could not even guess, at the basic contents of some of those heated platters, but it was a banquet out of his dreams.

When an unaccustomed sense of fullness put an end to his explorations, Nik came to himself again, to the uneasy realization that in accepting this bounty he had taken one more step along a trail that would lead him into very unfamiliar territory and that had its own dangers, perhaps the more formidable because they were unknown.

"Now"—Leeds pressed the return button and the table rolled away from them—"now, Nik, we talk."

3

But the captain did not begin. He was watching Nik with that same searching scrutiny the woman had turned on him earlier. And under that regard, as always, Nik squirmed, inwardly if not visibly. The boy had to call on strong will power to keep his hand away from his face.

"It's amazing!" Leeds might have been talking to himself. "Amazing!" he repeated. Then he came briskly to the point. "You must have gathered this is a Guild project?"

"Yes." Nik kept his answer short.

"That does not bother you?"

"In the Dipple you don't live by the law." Nik had never really tried to reason out his stand before, but that statement was true. Those in the Dipple had a brooding resentment of the in-powers who had long since condemned them to that forgotten refuse heap because they could neither protest nor fight back. There were three ways a man could escape the Dipple, and two of those had been closed to Nik from the beginning.

He could not possibly hope to hire out to any businessman on Korwar, and he could not ship in deep sleep to be sold as a laborer on another world. But the fact that he was now allied with the Thieves' Guild did not bother him at all. In a world—or a life—turned permanently against Nik Kolherne, any ally was to be welcomed.

"You have the proper attitude," Leeds conceded.

"Gyna thinks she can give you a new face. And if she thinks so, you can just about count on it."

"Gyna?"

"The Gentle Fem you just met. She's a cosmetic surgeon of the first rank."

"That tri-dee cast—I'm to look like that?" Nik ventured.

He had heard of the cosmetic surgeons and the wonders they were able to perform for fees impossible for an ordinary man to calculate. That one was tied to the Guild was perfectly in keeping with all else rumored about that shadowy empire. But it still remained something not to be believed that he could ever resemble that picture. Now Nik added a second question before Leeds had replied to the first.

"Who is he—that man in the tri-dee?"

"Someone who has life but no body," Leeds replied cryptically. He had a drowsy, satisfied look, as if he were content, satisfied in a way that had no relation to the food he had just eaten. "Yes, life—and we hope you'll provide the body."

Nik's imagination leaped. "Parasite!" He tensed again. There *were* some things worse than his face, and his fantasybred thoughts could supply a list of them.

Leeds laughed. "Give you the horrors, Nik? No, this is no monster rally. You're not being set up to provide a carcass for some other life type to move in. You're just going to be a dream, a hero out of a dream."

Completely baffled, Nik waited. Better let Leeds tell it his own way. If the captain did carry out his promise, Nik would owe him more than his life.

"Don't suppose at your age you pay much attention to politics." Leeds settled back on the divan. He took out his box again and began to suck one of the pellets from it. He did not wait for the boy to reply.

"The late war ended more or less as a draw—the fighting, that is. Then a real struggle started around the peace table when terms were offered, bargained for, schemed over. No one got as much as he wanted and most of them enough less to leave sores on their hides as tender as blaster burns. We're still at war in a way, though it's behind-the-scenes action now—not sending in ships and men and burning off a world here and there. And the Guild's for hire in some tricks for either side."

That made sense to Nik. On the lower levels, the Thieves' Guild might deal in ways that had given it its title, but in the upper strata, there were services such a band of outlaws could offer the heads of governments, sector lords, who would pay very well indeed.

"We've such a ploy on now, but it's been hanging fire because we needed a front for the first move."

"That's me?" Nik asked.

"That may be you," Leeds corrected. "And this is the truth." He still wore the half smile, but his eyes held no humor at all. "There will be no out once you begin."

"I guessed that."

"All right—then here's the full course. A year ago a warlord of one of the Nebula worlds sent his only son here to Korwar, just so pressure couldn't be brought on him through the boy. He picked one of the High Security villas, and that was that."

An HS villa was one that no unauthorized person could enter and that held its inhabitants safe as if they had been sealed in a double-illumi plate.

"Two months ago," Leeds continued, "the warlord ceased to be of any concern."

"Dead?" Nik was not surprised at Leeds' nod.

"Now the boy is no longer important as a hostage, but he is important for what he controls. Locked in his mind is the answer to a time-secure device that only he and his father knew. And behind the device are tapes that have information—of no value to the boy but of vast importance to two different parties. The one in power at present chooses to keep him under wraps— maybe for life. The other—"

"Wants him out," Nik finished.

"Yes. But they can't get him except by coming to us."

"And the Guild can crack an HS?"

"They could have cracked it any time within the past

year. That doesn't mean they could get the boy out. His father took every precaution. He has been blocked against any stranger, even one altered physically into a copy of a friend. He also has a circuit set in his brain. Force him or frighten him, and the information we need is totally wiped out."

"Then how?—" Nik was intrigued.

A small tri-dee scene, vividly real in spite of its size, glowed there. The landscape of the background was none that Nik had ever seen before. Rugged black heights were stark against a yellowish sky, and black sand lay level at their foot. Milky liquid flowed there in a crooked course. At the edge of that flood, the same dark-haired figure Nik had been shown by Gyna was down on one knee, engaged in skinning some reptilian creature.

The yellow light made a dazzling sparkle of parts of his clothing where metal overlays were fastened to a form of space uniform, but his head was bare and noticeable. Standing watching him was a much younger boy wearing a similar uniform. His hair was also black, and his hands grasped a weapon, a small edition of a blaster. His attitude was of one standing guard in dangerous territory. Leeds switched off the beam, and Nik waited for an explanation.

"Children cut off from normal friendships and lonely," the captain observed, "have a habit of imagining companions. Vandy Naudhin i'Akrama is no exception."

"Imagined companions," Nik repeated. "But that tri-dee showed two people—"

"What you saw was the fantasy Vandy has built up in his mind. He and his imagined companion-hero are not in the garden of the HS at all. They are on another world—I believe Vandy calls it Veever. Over a period of two years, he has been building up an elaborate fantasy existence that is most real to him now. And he lives in it for hours at a time."

"But how—?"

"How do we know this? How did we get this tape?"

Leeds shrugged. "Don't expect an explanation of the mechanics from me. The Guild has its resources. There are certain snooper-machines that have never been marketed, that are unknown to the public. None of the secrets men have sought to keep remain undiscovered. The Guild has the power to bid for such discoveries or take them. It remains that there *is* such a device, one that has snooped on Vandy's dream world for months and built up a complete file on his activities in that fantasy for our use."

"How?" Nik accepted Vandy's fantasy easily enough because of his own, but he still could not quite see how Leeds or the Guild proposed to use such a discovery for their purposes.

"Vandy has been blocked against all contact except through five people, two of whom are now dead," Leeds explained. "As far those who prepared him for this exile-protection know, there is no one now who dares to approach him without triggering the circuit that will erase instantly the knowledge we need. However, suppose Vandy *was* to meet, say in that particular portion of the HS garden where he feels most free from interruption, Hacon—"

"And Hacon is—?"

"You have just seen him, skinning a monster Vandy recognizes as an enemy on Veever. You will see him again as soon as possible, we all hope, in any mirror you care to glance into."

"So I meet Vandy as Hacon, and he tells me—" Nik began. The impossible was beginning to seem merely improbable.

But Leeds shook his head. "No, you meet Vandy and suggest an expedition—"

"Outside? Where?"

Leeds smiled lazily. "As to that, I can't give you any information. Since you are not an astro-navigator, anything I would tell you would make no sense. But you'll have an LB locked on a certain course. Once aboard, you and Vandy will go into stass. When you come out of that, you'll be where we want you."

"Off-world?"

"Off-world. In a place where we won't have to fear any chase. There you'll have time to consolidate your position with Vandy and get the information we need."

"And afterwards?"

"Afterwards, Vandy will be sent back here. You'll be a member in good standing in the Guild, with a face and a future. Nobody gets hurt except some politicos who've tried to gobble up more than they can safely swallow. In fact, Vandy will also have the satisfaction of tripping up a couple of those who helped to erase his father."

"But why off-world?"

"Because we *can* crack the HS, yes, but we can't preserve that crack for any length of time. You wouldn't have a chance to talk Vandy into any more than going with you. And we'll get you both off-world in a shielded LB because Vandy can be trailed by com-cast anywhere on Korwar. I told you his father took every precaution when he planted him here."

It made sense, and it could work, providing Gyna was able to turn Nik into Hacon. He thought of that smooth brown face, of Leeds' promise that that was what he might see in any mirror he cared to use. The price was a small one, and the reward—Nik drew a deep breath of wonder—the reward was out of one of his own cherished dreams.

"When do we start?" he asked eagerly.

Leeds hoisted his body off the divan and tucked his box of pills into his tunic. "Right now, Nik, right now."

Part of what followed Nik was to remember in sections that were hazier than his cherished fantasies. Most he was never to recall at all. And time had no meaning during this metamorphosis of Nik Kolherne into Hacon.

But there came an hour when he stood staring with incredulous wonder at a figure not on the wall this time but in a mirror, as Leeds had promised. And he was Hacon! A wild exhilaration filled him, and he

35

found himself laughing with a laughter that was close to chest-tearing sobs.

Leeds, who had brought him this miracle, stood there laughing, too, but more gently, before he nodded to Gyna.

"Well done, Gentle Fem." Leeds found words; Nik had none at all. But when he turned away from the mirror to face her, a little of his ecstasy was dampened by a vague apprehension because he could read no satisfaction in her expression.

She did not meet his gaze but glanced at Leeds, her soberness somehow a warning. And then she turned abruptly and left the room. Nik, puzzled, looked to the captain for enlightenment.

"What—?" And this time it was the other who would not meet Nik eye to eye.

He went back to the mirror, drew one hand down its glistening surface, and saw those fingertips meet the ones in the mirror reflection. So, that *was* he—no trickery there. But still something was wrong. His hand sought his face, not to mask it this time but to reassure himself by touch as well as by sight that there was firm brown skin there, flesh unscarred, bone no longer missing. He could see, he could feel—

"What is wrong?" Nik turned to stand before Leeds, making that demand with a fear all the keener because of his exhilaration of moments earlier.

"We had months to do a job that might have taken more than a year," Leeds said slowly, "three months lacking a few days. Gyna is not sure it will last unless"—now he did meet Nik's gaze—"unless you can get back into her hands within another two months, Korwar-planet time."

"But, you mean it will be the old story—no growth flesh—?" Nik dared not face his reflection again. That first blasting failure had occurred years ago, and he had been too young then to grasp the horror of what was happening. But now—now he would know!

"No," Leeds replied quickly, "this was done by another technique altogether. Gyna is sure it would have

36

succeeded with the right time element; now she cannot be sure. You may need a tightening process to recover any slip. But it will hold long enough for you to do the job. Then you'll come back here for the checkup."

"You'll swear to that?" Nik's rising fear was like a shaking sickness.

Leeds' hands held onto his shoulders. He stood tense and taut in that grip. "Nik, I'll swear by anything you want to name that we'll keep this promise, providing you deliver. The Guild takes care of its own."

There was enough truth in that to allay the icy fear a little. Nik knew the reputation of the organization—it was loyal to its own.

"All right. But in two months—"

"You'll have plenty of time. You start today, and you have all that you need right here." The captain lifted one hand from Nik's shoulder and tapped him in the middle of his forehead.

That was true. During the time he was being turned into Hacon outwardly, all the information gathered by snoopers had been fed into his mind by hypo-induction. Everything Vandy had created in Hacon and about Hacon was in Nik's mind, including the approach that would best entice Vandy into the needed adventure.

"When?"

"Right now," Leeds answered.

Nik had not been out of the suite of rooms for days, probably weeks, but the captain took him now with a sense of hurry that Nik's own need built. How long would Hacon last? Would he fail in his task and so lose everything? Yet the meeting with Vandy could not be too hurried; the boy's suspicions must not be aroused. Nik knew everything about Vandy that the snooper tapes could tell, but that did not mean he knew Vandy.

"You have all any induction can give you." Leeds did not sound in the least worried as they went down one of the long corridors that Nik knew were underground. "It's been so well planted in your mind that you can't make a wrong move, even if you wanted to. Just get him into the LB—"

"But when we get there—on that other planet?"

"No need to worry about that. The setup on Dis has been in order for months. You'll have all the help you need there."

They came out not on the roof of the gray-green house this time but on a hillside, where a cluster of rocks and a fringe of bushes had concealed the opening. There was a small glade in which a flitter waited, another man already aboard. That flier had an odd shimmer about its outline, a light that made Nik's eyes smart and forced him to look away quickly. Some other trick device for its concealment, he decided. Leeds climbed in and took the controls, proving that the flier was not on a set flight pattern.

"Set?" Leeds asked of the other passenger.

The man consulted the timekeeper on his wrist. His lips moved as if he counted; then he snapped his fingers, and on that signal the flitter bounced into the air under a full spurt of power. They were out of the masking greenery and flying into the wilderness beyond the fringe of the city.

"Correct course and speed," the man behind Leeds ordered. "Two—four—hold it!"

The flier bore on. They lifted over the first range of hills, and Nik looked down into the tangled mass of vegetation. Then he caught a glimpse of red stone walls surrounding a solid-looking building.

The flitter came about in order to approach the building from another direction.

"What about the LB?" Nik dared to ask. How could they have planted any craft as large as a space lifeboat undetected by the guards below?

"It's ready." Leeds appeared to have full confidence in that. "When, Jaj?"

"Now!"

The flitter gave a forward leap like the spring of a stalking beast upon its prey, coming down between trees. Leeds signaled Nik out through the hatch Jaj held open. He landed with a roll on thick and cushioning turf. As he scrambled to his feet, he looked up.

There was no sign of the flitter at all, nor could he hear a motor hum. So far Leeds was right. Nik was past the safeguards of the HS villa, only a few yards from the very point where the snooper had been planted in the beginning. Well, the captain had also said that the Guild Forecast Com had given 73 per cent odds on the success of this part of the plan.

Nik brushed down the fantastic spacer's uniform Vandy had created for Hacon and walked quietly forward. He stood between two drooping limbed bushes to look into a small hidden glade.

Someone was there before him, sitting down with knees hunched against his chest, his attention all for a hopping creature making erratic progress across the sod.

Nik came into the open. "Vandy?" he called.

4

Nik was crawling down a tunnel of cold dark, but ahead was an encouraging spark of light, a promise of warmth. The light closed in about him as he lay looking up at a rounding curve of blue, which held the hard, sleek sheen of metal. He blinked and tried to think clearly.

There was a chime ringing in his ears, growing more strident. He raised himself on one elbow, and the wink of a flashing light dazzled his eyes. This—this was the LB! And he was coming out of stass.

The chime—that meant they were nearing the end of the voyage. *They!* Nik sat up abruptly to look at the other bunk. Vandy lay there, still curled in sleep, his dark lashes shadows on his cheeks, the netting of take-off straps holding him in safety.

Nik's own straps were taut across his thighs. And the wink, the chime, were warning enough to stay where he was. He wriggled down and fastened the second belt. Coming in for a landing—but where?

Korwar was one of a six-planet system and the only inhabitable world in that system. And Leeds, while being evasive over their destination, had insisted that they need not fear pursuit. Probably their voyage had removed them not only from Korwar but from its sun as well. And to Nik, ignorant as he was of galactic courses, they could be anywhere, even on Vandy's Veever.

Vandy's Veever, Vandy's Hacon, Vandy's dream— Nik lay flat, waiting for the landing controls to take over, and thought about how right Leeds had been so far. From that moment when Vandy had looked up in the garden to see Nik standing in the open sunlight, he had accepted Nik unquestioningly. Nik squirmed now on the plasta-foam filled bunk. Too easy—this whole operation had begun. His hand twitched, but the straps prevented his raising it to his face, to feel tangible evidence of the change he accepted as a small part of truth, the one thing he clung to fiercely. And how long could he continue to cling? Leeds had said perhaps two months—

LB's were fashioned to rove wide courses in space. The very nature of those escape craft meant that they had to be almost equal to the fastest cruisers as they took the "jumps" in and out of hyper-space to carry out their rescue missions. But how much time had passed now? Nik had no idea of how long it had been since they had taken off from Korwar. Any minute the change in him might start—

His smooth lips twisted on a sound that was close to a moan. Leeds—surely Leeds would be waiting for their landing. Nik believed that Leeds was the leader in this Guild operation. But what if he wasn't there or if he did not have power enough to make good on his promise? And how long would it take to learn from Vandy the information they wanted? Even if the boy had accepted Nik easily as an adventure companion, would he share something he had been taught to keep secret? The holes in the future became bigger and blacker all the time!

With a final clang, the chime stilled, and Nik was aware of the increasing discomfort of landfall. His past traveling on ships had been long ago, and now he was conscious of the strain on his body, though an LB, which might be transporting injured, was rigged with every possible protection against pressure.

"Hacon!" The cry shrilled with a sharp undertone of fear and made Nik force his head to one side on the bunk. Across the narrow space between them, he saw Vandy's eyes wide open, the fear in them.

"All—right—" Nik got out the words of assurance. "We're setting down—"

Then he felt the surge of the deter-rockets, and the weight of change brought him close to the edge of a complete blackout.

They were down, a smooth three-fin landing he judged, though his knowledge of such was very meager. Wriggling one arm loose from the straps, Nik pushed the button on the side wall and looked up expectantly at the visa-plate for the first glimpse of the new world. And in spite of all the worries nibbling at him, there was a small thrill of excitement in waiting to see what lay outside the skin of the LB.

Dark—darker than the blackest night on Korwar— with a faint glimmer in the distance. But such dark!

"Hacon—where—where are we?" Vandy's voice was thin, shaken.

"On Dis." At least Leeds had supplied him with a name. But where Dis was remained another matter.

"Dis—" the boy repeated. "Hacon—what are we going to do here?"

Nik unbuckled his straps, sat up, and reached across to do the same for Vandy. "We"—he tried to make his voice express the proper authority—"are going to have an adventure."

"The Miccs—they're hunting again?"

The Miccs—those were Vandy's ever-present, ever-to-be-battled enemies. But no use in Nik's building what he might not be able to deliver, well-versed as he was in Vandy's fantasy world.

"This is just a scouting trip," he replied. "I don't know whether they are here or not."

"Hacon—look! Something's coming!"

Nik glanced at the visa-plate. There was movement there, the on-and-off flash of what might be a torch, and it was advancing toward the LB. He helped Vandy from the bunk and drew the boy with him to the escape lock at the end of the small compartment, but he made no move to open that until he heard the tapping from without.

Air poured in—humid, hot, with a sweetish, almost gagging odor, as if it had blown across a stretch of rotting vegetation. It was cloying, clogging in the nostrils. Vandy coughed.

"That smells bad," he commented rather than complained.

"All right?" The inquiry came from without. The light from the LB port showed a man, his face, raised to view them, half masked with large goggles. "Here." A hand reached to Nik, and obediently he took the ends of two lines, both made fast to the welcomer's belt. "Tie those on," he was ordered. "This is no place to be lost!"

The humidity of the dark beyond was so oppressive that Nik was already bathed in perspiration, and he breathed shallowly, as if a weight rested above his laboring lungs. He knotted one cord to his own belt, one to Vandy's, and then dropped from the lock hatch, lifting down the boy.

"This way—" Their guide had already melted into the all-enveloping dark, towing them behind him. Luckily, he did not walk fast, and the ground under their feet appeared reasonably smooth. Vandy pressed against Nik, and the latter kept hold of the smaller boy's shoulder.

As they moved away from the lights of the LB, more features of the dark landscape became clearer. Here and there were faint halos of misty radiance outlining a large rock, a weird-seeming bush—or at least a growth that had the general appearance of a bush. But for the rest, it was all thick black, and when Nik turned his eyes to the sky, not a single gleam of a star broke the brooding blackness. Always the rotten stench was in their nostrils, and the humidity brought drops of moisture rolling in oily beads across their skin.

"Hacon—" Vandy was only a small body moving under Nik's hand, not to be seen in this night-held steambath. "Why doesn't that man use his torch?"

For the first time, Nik's attention was drawn from their weird surroundings to the guide. Vandy was right; they had seen the flicker of a torch when the stranger had approached the LB, but since they had left the ship, he had not used it. Yet he moved through the soupy blackness with the confidence of one who could see perfectly. Those goggles? But why link his two companions to him by towlines? Why not simply use a torch and show them the way?

The lines became for Nik not a matter of convenience but a symbol of dependence, which was disquieting. He stepped up, bringing Vandy with him and closing the gap between them and their guide.

"How about using your torch? This is a dark night."

To Nik's amazement, the answer was a laugh and then the words, "Night? This is the middle of the day!"

If that was meant to confuse him, Nik thought, it did.

"First day I ever saw that was a complete blackout," he retorted sharply.

"Under an infrared sun," the other replied, "this is all you'll ever see."

Nik was puzzled. His education had been a hit-or-miss—mostly miss—proposition, so the guide's explanation was meaningless. But Vandy apparently understood.

"That's why you're wearing cin-goggles then," he stated rather than questioned.

"Right," the stranger began, and then his voice arose in a shouted order. "Down! Get down!"

Nik flung himself forward, taking Vandy with him, so that they rolled across a hard surface on which evil-smelling, slimy things smeared to pulp under their weight. Their guide was using the torch now, sending its beam in a spear shaft of light to impale in the glare a winged thing of which they could see only nightmare portions. Then the beam of a blaster cut up and out, and there was a curdling scream of pain and fury as the blackened mass of the attacker whirled on, already charred and dead, to fall heavily some distance away.

Again their guide laughed. "Just one of the local

hunters," he told them. "But you see that planet-side walks are not to be recommended. Now, let's get going. There're going to be some more arrivals soon; they don't get a chance to dine on flapper very often." Jerking at the towlines, he hurried them along.

They were going on a downslope, Nik knew, and walls of stone were rising higher on either side. But whether those were purposeful erections or native cliffs, he had no idea. He did see at one backward glance that, where their boots had crushed the ground growths, there were small ghostly splotches of phosphorescence with an evil greenish glow marking their back trail.

But even if he and Vandy could regain the LB, the ship would not lift. The controls had been locked in a pattern to bring them here, and Nik had neither the knowledge of a course to take them home or the ability to reset the controls. Home? Korwar—the Dipple— His hand went to his face. What lay behind him was *not* home! And why did he wish to backtrack? The action, as Leeds had outlined it, was simple enough. Vandy accepted him without question, and to the boy this would be only a very real adventure straight out of his fantasy world. He would be induced to share with Hacon the information Leeds or his superiors wanted. Then Vandy would go home, and he, Nik, would have earned his pay. He knew from his briefing what Vandy had made of Hacon and what he would have to do to sustain his role. Only, in these surroundings, with their total and frightening alienness, could Nik Kolherne be Hacon long? Already he was baffled by information Vandy knew and he did not, and he would be a prisoner wherever they were going until he gained some manner of sight. He was sure that this was a planet on which Terran stock were total aliens and where every danger was to be fronted without much preparation on his part.

But once he saw Leeds—Nik held tightly to that thought. Leeds was the stable base in this whole affair and meant security.

Without warning, there gaped before them a slit of

light, which grew wider as they approached it. Then they passed through and into a rock-hewn chamber, for that was what it was, not a natural cave. A click behind them signaled the closing of the door.

The humid, sickly air of the outside was thinned by a cooler, fresher current, and their guide shed his goggles. He was a stocky, thick-set man, with the deep browning of a space crewman, like any to be seen portside at Korwar. Now he stepped into an alcove in the wall and stood while a mist curled out and wreathed about him. In a moment he came out and waved Nik and Vandy to take his place.

"What for?" Vandy wanted to know.

"So you don't take them inside." A crook of thumb indicated the floor.

There were the smears from their boots, and in those smears tiny lumps were rising. One branched in three—waving arms? Branches? Tentacles? A quick-growing thing from smears. Nik shivered. That flying creature their guide had killed he could accept, but these were different. He took firm hold of Vandy and shoved the boy in before him so that they huddled together in the alcove, sniffing a bracing air that carried a spicy, aromatic odor, the very antithesis of the humid reek outside this chamber.

Beyond the entrance, they found themselves in a barracks-like series of corridors and rooms, all hollowed in rock, mostly empty of either people or furnishings. They passed only two other men, both wearing space uniforms, both as nondescript as their guide.

Nik sensed a growing restlessness in Vandy. None of this resembled the dream adventures he and Hacon had shared in the past. Nor, Nik realized, was his own passive part akin to the figure Vandy had built up in his imagination. Nik had promised him an adventure, and this was far from the boy's conception of that.

"In here!" A jerk of the head sent the two of them past their guide into another room. This was manifestly designed as living quarters, with a bunk against the far wall, a fold-up table, and a couple of stools. The air current sighed overhead at intervals, coming through a slit no wider than the edge of Nik's hand. When he turned quickly, the door had closed, and he did not have to be told that they were prisoners. He pressed against the slide panel just to make sure of that point, but the barrier held.

"Hacon!" Vandy stood in the middle of the room, his fists on his hips, his small face sober with a frown. "This—this is real!"

"It's real." Nik could understand the other's momentary bewilderment. He had fashioned fantasies, too. And when he had fallen captive to Leeds' weapon in the warehouse, been freed from the Dipple, and gained what he had wanted most—why, at times all of that had seemed just part of a dream. But there had been moments of awareness, of doubt—and those were more than fleeting moments now. If Leeds had been here, if Nik had been told more of what to expect—

"Hacon, I want to go home!" That was a demand. Vandy's scowl was dark. "If you don't take me home, I'll—"

Nik sat down on the nearest stool. "You'll what?" he asked wearily.

"I'll call Umar." Vandy fumbled with the mid-seal fastening that covered a carry pocket in the breast of his tunic. He brought out a glistening object, which he held on the flat of his palm and studied with concentration. A moment later he looked up. "It doesn't work!" The scowl of impatience was fading. "But Father will find me; he'll bring the guard—"

Hadn't they told Vandy his father was dead? Nik's fingers picked at the broad belt with its fringe of weapons and tools that Vandy had thought up for his created hero. There were plenty of those. It was a pity they didn't have the powers Vandy had endowed them with—or would some one of them provide him with a weapon, a tool, so that he would not have to wait passively for trouble?

Why did he expect trouble, one part of Nik's brain demanded even as he began to pull that collection of show armament out for examination? Because he had been set down on a world where he was blinded among sighted men? Because he was limited by lack of information and driven by a feeling that there was little time?

"This is real, Vandy," he said slowly. "But it's an adventure, one we'll take together." If only Vandy hadn't build Hacon up as invincible! How was he going to keep Vandy believing in him? And if Vandy learned the truth, then the chances of getting what Leeds wanted sank past the vanishing point. And if he, Nik, could not deliver—

He was holding a small rod in his hand, one that was tipped with a disk of shining metal. In Vandy's imagination, it could generate a heat ray to cut through stone or metal. Now it served Nik as a mirror to reflect the smooth face he still did not dare to accept. If Nik Kolherne did not, and speedily, keep his part of the bargain, could he hope to keep that? He had to get Vandy's knowledge, and he could do it only by preserving Vandy's image of him—or rather of Hacon. Which meant that his own doubts must be stifled, that he must make a game of all this.

"Why are we here?" To Nik's ears, that held a note of suspicion.

"They think that they have us." Nik improvised hurriedly. "But really we came because your father is going to follow us—he can trace you, you know. And then at the right moment, we'll get him in. Then the Miccs will be taken—"

"No!" Vandy's shake of the head was decisive. "These aren't Miccs—are they, Hacon? It's Lik Iskhag's doing! And how are we going to help anyone if they keep us shut up? If Umar tells Father and they come to get us—maybe it's all a trap and Father and Umar will be taken, too! We have to get out of here! You get us out quick, Hacon!"

48

None of this was promising. Nik shoved the "heat ray" back in its belt loop. With Vandy in his present mood, Nik would never be able to talk him into telling what Leeds wanted. And Iskhag—that was the blue-skinned alien on Korwar. But Vandy wasn't of the same race. How did Iskhag fit into the picture or into the story Leeds had detailed for Nik?

"Listen, Vandy. I can't work blind, you know. Remember when we went hunting for the jewels of Caraska? We had to have information such as those map tapes we found in the derelict ship, and we had to learn the Seven Words of Sard." Feverishly, Nik delved into past Hacon adventures. "Now I have to know other things."

"What things?" There was a note of hostility in that, Nik believed.

"You're helping your father, aren't you, Vandy? Keeping some information for him?"

When the boy shook his head, Nik was not too surprised. Whatever had been left in Vandy's brain under the drastic safeguards Leeds had described was not going to be extracted easily.

"Why else would Iskhag want you?" He tried a slightly different approach.

"Bait—to get my father!" Vandy replied promptly.

"Why? What does Iskhag have against your father?"

"Because Warlord Naudhin i'Akrama"—there was a vast pride in Vandy's answer—"is going to hold Glamsgog until the end. And Lik Iskhag wants the Inner Places—"

The reply had no meaning for Nik at all. And why didn't Vandy know his father was dead? Had that been kept a secret from him for pity or for policy?

"If Father comes here and Iskhag gets him," Vandy continued, "then—then Glamsgog will be gone and every one of the Guardians will be killed! We have to get away before that happens—we have to!"

Vandy pushed past Nik and set his palms against

49

the sliding surface of the door. His small shoulders grew stiff with the effort he was making to force it open. "We have to!" he panted, and his fear was plain to hear.

5

"Vandy!" Nik made that sharp enough to attract the boy's attention. "When did pounding on walls ever open a door?" He was working by instinct now. Hypo-tapes had made him part of Vandy's fantasy world; he knew that to the smallest detail. But with Vandy himself, beyond that imagination, rich and creative as it was, he trod unknown territory. How much dared he appeal to the boy's good sense?

He did not even know Vandy's real age. Various branches of once Terran stock had mutated and adapted so that a life span might vary from seventy to three hundred years. Vandy could be a boy of ten or twelve; also he might be twice that and still be a child. And Nik realized that the perilous gaps in his own information concerning his companion were dangerous. Surely Leeds could not have intended this companionship to endure for any length of time.

Vandy had come away from the door to face Nik. There was a shadow on his small face, but his jaw was set determinedly.

"We have to get out."

"Yes." Nik could echo that. "But not without a plan—" He grabbed at the one delaying suggestion that might not only give him time to think a little but might also produce information from Vandy. To his vast relief, the boy nodded and sat down on the other stool.

"Once we're out of this room"—Nik took the first difficulty that came to mind—"we can't manage without goggles."

51

"That man had them," Vandy pointed out. "We'll need blasters, too. That flying thing—there may be more of those."

"All right. But even with goggles and blasters, we can't go back to the LB—that was set on a locked course." Nik was listing the problems. "But just what we can do—"

Nik, sensitive without being conscious of it to some change in the atmosphere, glanced at Vandy. His eyes were normally golden, but now there seemed to be sparks of red fire in their depths. His small face was expressionless.

"You aren't—" he began when Nik made a sudden warning gesture.

Behind Vandy, the door panel was opening. Nik arose to face it.

The same crewman who had brought them here tossed some ration containers in the general direction of the flap table. One missed and rolled to Vandy's feet. He stooped to pick it up.

"I want to see Captain Leeds," Nik said quickly.

"He ain't here."

"When will he come?"

"When he's sent for, unless he gets some big ideas and makes the jump on his own."

"Then who's in charge?" Nik persisted. If Leeds was not, what did that mean for him, for Vandy, for the whole plan?

"Orkhad. And he wants to see you now. No—the kid stays here," he added as Nik motioned to Vandy.

"I'll be back," Nik promised, but Vandy's level gaze, still holding that ruddy spark, did not change. He said nothing as Nik hesitated irresolutely.

"Come on. Orkhad's not a Veep as takes kindly to waiting," the crewman said.

Nik went, but his first uneasiness was now a definite dislike of both his surroundings and the situation here. As they went down the corridor, he surveyed the physical features of the place. The walls were rock, hollowed out, not built up by blocks. Though the current of air was fresh, there were slimy trickles of moisture marking their surfaces. Who had fashioned this place Nik did not know, but he was convinced it was not the present inhabitants.

There were several chambers opening off that hall, all fitted with metal doors far newer than the walls on which they were installed. From quick glances, Nik learned those other rooms were living quarters, all like the one where he had been with Vandy.

They passed a larger room with a rack of blasters on the wall and various storage boxes piled within. Then the hall ended in large space dimly lighted. They threaded their way along a narrow balcony hanging above a wide space in which at least a dozen passages met in star formation, as if this were a grand terminal of some vast transportation system. But there was nothing to be seen in the half gloom save all those tunnel mouths evenly spaced about the expanse of the chamber.

The balcony brought them into another corridor, and Nik sniffed a new scent on the air. He had known that on Korwar. Someone not too far away was or had lately been smoking suequ weed.

Holding some of the same sickliness that seemed to be a part of the natural air of this world, the aroma grew stronger as they neared the end of the second corridor. And with every breath Nik drew, his fear grew. Suequ weed was one of the many drugs mankind had discovered to rot body and mind, and its side effects made for real trouble. The smoker lost all sense of fear or prudence, any sane balance of judgment. And the drug fostered recklessness that could involve not only the user but also his companions, were he in any position to give orders. If this Orkhad was the suequ smoker—

The room at the end of the corridor was different, in that an attempt had been made to lend it a measure of comfort. There was a strip of matting across the floor and a cover of black feathers fluffing from the bunk. Fastened to the wall above that was a picture—not tri-dee but rather a round of crystal in which were suspended a number of brightly hued creatures, either insects or birds.

Oddly enough, the smell of suequ was not so strong in the room, though the empty pipe lay on the table to the right of the man sitting there, turning around in his fingers a cup that was a barbaric art of precious metal and roughly cut gems.

He was plainly of Iskhag's race, though his present dress was far removed from the other's foppish splendor. His tunic was well cut but bare of ornament, and there was not so much as a jeweled buckle on his belt. Hs boots were those of any spaceman, though new, and the over-all color of his clothing was a russet brown. He was not armed, though the hooks of a blaster hold were riveted to his belt.

Nik's guide sketched a casual salute and took his place against the wall, leaving his charge in the open to face Orkhad. The alien did not break the silence, and Nik, wondering if the other were trying to needle him into some impatient mood, held to the same quiet.

Then Orkhad suddenly brought his cup down on the table top, the metal against metal producing a ringing note.

"You"—the thin notes of his high voice had a monotonous sound— "what do you do?"

To Nik, the question made very little sense. His job had been clearly defined back on Korwar. He was to bring Vandy here—wherever in the galaxy "here" was—and wheedle out of the boy the information Leeds needed.

"More of Leeds' work!" Without waiting for any reply, Orkhad spat out that name, making it sound like an obscene oath. "Why did you come? To put the boy in the ship was all that was necessary. We are not so well-supplied that we can feed extra mouths. You are not needed here."

"That isn't what Captain Leeds said. I do not have the information yet—"

Orkhad only stared at Nik. The eyes in that blue face

slitted instead of widened, as if the alien narrowed vision to see the better.

"Information?" he repeated. "What is this information?"

"Captain Leeds gave me my orders."

"And Captain Leeds"—Orkhad made mockery of the name and title with the first real inflection Nik had heard in his voice—"is not here. He may not be here for some time. Here I am Veep—do you understand? And it is for me to determine the orders given—and obeyed. You have brought us Warlord Naudhin i'Akrama's son. That is well. For him we have a use. And this is a world that is all your enemy. Do you understand that?

"It has a sun in the sky right enough—a red dwarf sun whose rays you cannot see, not with *your* eyes. I can see a little, but your breed can see nothing unless you wear cins. And it is a world to which things have happened—for it is close to its dark sun. Sometime—who knows how long ago—there was a flare that crisped out to make of this planet a scorched thing. Its seas were steamed into vapor, which still clouds overhead, though a measure of this comes earthward in rainstorms such as you cannot conceive of.

"There was life here before that flare. This"—one of those blue hands indicated the walls about them—"was perhaps a refuge wrought in despair by some intelligent life form long before Captain Leeds' friends homed in here to discover a base to serve us well. Yes, intelligence burrowed and squirmed, hoping to preserve life, only to be burned away. So now we have some life, but none we cannot master with a blaster. Only to venture out into that murk without cin-goggles, without weapons—that is death as certain as its sun once gave this planet. Do you understand that?"

Nik nodded.

"So, we are agreed. This base, it is life; out there is death. And in this base it is by my will that life continues. Since the boy knows you, will be quiet with you, you shall continue to be with him until we are ready to deal with him. That small purpose you may serve. Fabic, take him away."

Nik went, adding up small items. Fabic was matching him step for step, and when they reached the balcony above the terminal, the crewman spoke.

"I never saw you with the captain."

"I wasn't one of his crew."

Fabic grinned. "So you wasn't of his crew. That figures—you'd have to be some older to make that claim. But you are his man now, and so I'll pass on a warning. Don't know when the captain will fin in here, but until he does, Orkhad gives the orders. You remember that, and there'll be no flamer to push you out of orbit."

"I have orders from Captain Leeds about the boy."

Fabic shrugged. "All right then, stall—and you'd better be smart about it, too. Let Orkhad get another pipe into him, and he's liable to try his luck at taking over. Then it wouldn't matter much what orders you had from the captain."

"You're a Leeds man?" Nik couldn't help that one question that might mean so much.

Fabic still grinned. "Me, I'm playing it safe—all the way safe! This is no planet to go exploring on. And I don't aim to be set outside without cin-goggles and a blaster and told to start walking! That has happened before. Sure, I'll back the captain—*if* he's here and ready to speak up. But I'm not stripping myself bare for him regardless. If you want to spit in Orkhad's eye, you'll do it on your own and take what he'll give you then all by yourself. Walk slow and soft and forget you know how to speak until the captain does show—"

"Which will be when?"

"When it suits him. Here's your hole. Crawl right in and remember to be invisible when trouble comes—"

Still trying to make something coherent out of those hints, Nik re-entered the cell-like chamber and heard Fabic click the door behind him. Vandy still sat on his stool, staring at an unopened tin of emergency space rations.

56

That gave Nik an idea for putting off explanations for a while.

"Let's eat!" He set the button for heating and, opening the nearest container, handed it to the boy.

When it popped open and the steam arose from its interior, Nik realized that he too was hungry. Vandy looked mulishly stubborn for a second or two, but it seemed that he could not resist that aroma either. They ate in silence, savoring the food. Nik counted the pile of containers Fabic had brought—enough for three days, maybe more. Did that mean they would be imprisoned here for that length of time or merely that Fabic did not want to make too many trips to supply them?

Leeds was coming, but, meanwhile, with Orkhad in command and hostile— What if the alien Veep moved against Vandy and incidentally against Nik?

How big were these underground diggings? That terminal with its radiating star of tunnels suggested size. Was Orkhad right? Were all these corridors, rooms, tunnels, part of a refuge system developed by a native race in a despairing attempt to survive the flare from their sun, an attempt that had failed? Did Orkhad have any large force here, enough to occupy an extensive section? If Nik only knew more!

Supplies for three days—and those tunnels. Nik's thoughts kept juggling those two facts, trying to add them as if he could make a satisfactory sum. As long as Leeds was not here, Orkhad was in control. Their safety rested on the very shaky foundation of the whims of a suequ smoker.

"I want to go home—" Vandy put down the empty ration tin. There was no panic now as he had shown earlier. But Nik, occupied though he was with his thoughts, read the determination in the boy's tone.

"We can't go." He was startled into a bald statement of truth.

"I will go!" Vandy sped across the room before Nik could move. He fitted his small fingers into the door slit, and the panel gave!

Nik launched himself at the boy to drag him back, while Vandy fought like a cornered dra-cat. Holding him on the bunk by the sheer weight of his own body, Nik strove to reason with his captive.

"All right, all right," he repeated. "Only we can't just walk out of here."

Why was the door left unfastened? Had Fabic overlooked that precaution on purpose or in carelessness? Did the crewman's weak allegiance to Leeds take that way out, giving Nik and Vandy an offer of escape? Or was it intended to be a method of getting rid of them both, organized by Orkhad?

Vandy lay quiet now, the red sparks blazing in his eyes.

Supplies, arms, cin-goggles—the tunnels—a chance to hide out until Leeds did arrive? It was wild, so wild that Nik could only consider such a plan because the fear that had been rising in him since their landing on Dis was now an icy and constant companion. He was sure that whatever plan Leeds had made had gone wholly awry, and the next move might be his alone.

"Listen!" Still keeping the tight grip pinning Vandy to the bunk, Nik spoke hurriedly. "We can't use the LB, but they must have other ships or a ship here. And Captain Leeds is coming. If we can hide out until he arrives, then everything will be all right. There are some tunnels—" Quickly, he outlined what he had seen during the trip to Orkhad's quarters.

"We need cin-goggles." Vandy's face was no longer closed and hard.

"We won't go outside!" Nik was determined on that.

"The goggles will be better to use than a torch in the dark," Vandy returned. "And if there is a ship, then we'll have to go out to reach it."

Back in the Dipple, Nik had spun his own adventures, neat pieces of dreamed action wherein all the major advantages had been his. But to start out blindly in the real thing was very different. He wondered fleetingly if Vandy found this true also. Superficially, this was not so different from the fantasies the boy had woven about Hacon and himself in that Korwarian garden, but Nik was not Hacon and this was no dream adventure.

"Blankets—" He might as well start off practically. Nik swept the supply tins from the table, bundled the coverings on the bunk around them, and secured everything into an awkward package with his belt. He was tempted to discard that fringe of mock weapons and tools but finally decided against that with the faint hope that some one of those might prove valuable after all.

Just how they were to obtain cin-goggles he had no idea, but blasters were racked in that room down the corridor. And with a blaster, he would feel less like a naked cor worm exposed to the day when the cover rock of its sleep chamber was torn away.

Inch by inch, Nik worked open the door. There was no change in the light of the walls. As far as Nik could see, the doors of the other chambers ahead were just as he had viewed them last, one or two half open, the rest closed. He signaled Vandy to silence and tried to hear any small noise that might herald waiting trouble. There was no sound, and he motioned Vandy out into the corridor and silently eased the door shut.

The bundle he carried by the belt fastening provided a weapon of sorts, always supposing he was the one to surprise a newcomer. At least, it was the only protection they had. With his fingers locked in that strap hold, Nik edged out into the corridor, Vandy between him and the wall.

They reached the first of those half-open doors. Vandy jerked at the edge of Nik's tunic and pointed. They could both see the strap, the round lenses. A set of goggles lay on the tip table in there. But most of the room, the bunk itself, was hidden. Suppose it was occupied? To get those goggles meant taking three, four steps in—

Before Nik could stop him, Vandy was on his way. Just inside, he stiffened, and Nik raised the bundle. The room *was* occupied! He dared not move to pull the boy back for fear of alerting the occupant. But Vandy—surely Vandy had sense enough to withdraw.

Nik bit his lips. Vandy was not retreating as his companion so fiercely willed him to. Instead, he squatted close to floor level, his attention all for something well to Nik's left and completely out of his range of vision. Then Vandy began to crawl on hands and knees, his body as close to the floor as he could manage. Helpless, Nik was forced to watch.

Now Vandy was directly below the table, his hand rising to the strap. Nik's heart pounded, so that the blood in his ears was a heavy beat. He had heard that snuffling, the rustle of bunk coverings as if the occupant stirred. Vandy's hand was motionless, his head turned. Nik could see one eye, very watchful. Then his hand moved down, and his fingers closed in triumph on the strap.

6

Seconds stretched into nerve-racking minutes. Vandy hitched his way out of the room, the goggles clasped tight to his chest. He was at the door, getting to his feet again. Nik set aside the bundle, and his hands closed on the boy, jerking him back and out of what could have been a trap.

He looked down into Vandy's face. The boy's eyes were alight, his lips curved in a wide smile, but Nik did not respond. He pulled Vandy away from the door.

"Don't ever try anything like that again!" He thinned his whisper to the merest thread of sound, his lips close to Vandy's ear.

Vandy was still grinning. "Got 'em!" He dangled the goggles.

"And whoever was in there could have gotten you!" Nik retorted. "No more chances—"

Teaming with Vandy was trouble. Nik had been transformed into Hacon outwardly, but for a human being to resemble the imagined hero of a small boy was almost impossible. In the fantasy adventures of Hacon and Vandy, Vandy had always had equality of action. If Nik tried to impose the need for caution on the boy now, it might end in a clash of wills that would imperil their escape. Feverishly Nik searched his Hacon memory for some precedent that would render Vandy more amenable to his orders in the immediate future.

"This is a Silcon job." He brought out the best argument he could muster. "A slip will mean failure, Vandy."

"All right. But I did get the goggles! And we'll have to get another pair, won't we?"

"If we can." Privately Nik thought that their picking up the first pair had been such a piece of good luck that it was unlikely that such an opportunity would occur again. He recalled Leeds' belief in luck but was not moved to accept that belief for his own. To acquire one pair of goggles without mishap was perhaps all they dared hope to do.

The soft whish-whish of the air current over their heads was the only sound in the corridor. Nik counted doors to locate the room where he had seen the arms rack. Once both of them paused as a mutter from another sleeping chamber suggested the occupant was awake or waking. Nik was somewhat appeased by Vandy's present sober expression and his quiet.

At the arms room, they were faced by a closed door, which did not yield to Nik's efforts to slide it back. But the thoughts of the blasters kept him busy past the first sharp disappointment. To venture out into the unknown dangers of the tunnels without weapons was too perilous. He had too good a memory of that winged thing that had attacked outside the refuge. Perhaps other native creatives had found their way underground. Neither did he want to face any pursuit of Orkhad's forces with empty hands.

Nik's fingers traced the crack of the door. It did not give in the slightest to his urging. He turned the supply bundle around in his hands, examining those glittering "weapons" still in the belt loops. They could not deliver the power Vandy had imagined for them, but in their shapes and sizes, there might be one to answer his purpose now.

He chose the mirror ray and worked its curved edge into the door crack at the position of the locking mechanism. It was not a finger-heat seal, for which Nik was thankful, and his probing did meet obstruction. Carefully he began to pry, levering the mirror edge back and forth, so that it moved more freely.

Nik applied more pressure. His position was awkward, and he could not bring much weight to bear. But at last there was a click, and the door moved. A locked door should mean an empty room, and it was dark. Swiftly, Nik grasped the goggles, not sure they would work.

But they did, and he was able to see in an odd fashion, enough to make sure that the room was empty of all except its stark furnishing and the arms rack. He motioned Vandy in with him.

Four blasters stood in the rack slots. Nik took the first and saw that the dial butt indicated a full charge. At least Orkhad's men kept their arms in order. He thrust the weapon into the front of his tunic. Vandy reached for the second in the rack. Nik was about to protest and then kept silent. Whether Vandy could use the arm or not, a second one would be worth taking. Nik slipped the two remaining out of the rack, set their beams on full, and laid them on the floor. With any luck, they would lie there undiscovered until their charges were completely exhausted. It would take time to recharge them.

Luck again—he was beginning to think as Leeds did. And why was he so sure that the men here in the refuge were his enemies? Nik returned to the present problem, that of getting away from the quarters of Orkhad's force.

Vandy was staring, fascinated, at the wall beginning to glow red from the force beams. What effect that disintegration might have Nik did not know, but he shouldered the pack and pushed the boy back to the corridor. Outside, he shut the door once again and inserted in the crack another of the belt "tools," twisting the narrow strip of metal well into the slot and then melting it with his new weapon to make sure. That was a new door lock that would take them some time to break.

They came out on the balcony above the terminal of the tunnels. What if there was no way down? The expanse above that star-shaped convergence was big and shadowed. Nik could make out a matching balcony on the opposite side as he came to the edge to look over. There was nothing moving below, no sign that Orkhad's people had any use for that series of rock-hewn ways. Nik measured the drop with his eyes and then went to work.

The contents of the bundle were spread out and two of the covers knotted together. Yes, that ought to reach.

"We climb down?" Vandy whispered.

"No, I'll lower you, then drop—" Nik tested the knots with hard jerks, listening all the while for any intimation that their escape had been discovered. Was the scent of suequ stronger? Had Orkhad gone back to the pipe? Nik fastened one blanket end to Vandy and helped the boy clamber over the rail.

He played out the improvised line and saw the pale face turned up to him as Vandy signaled safe arrival. Now up with the rope again. A bag was made of it to lower the supply containers. The whole thing dropped. Not too far away there was a rise in the surface of the tunnel level, close to Orkhad's quarters. Nik measured that distance by eye. To approach that end of the balcony was an added risk, but it was his best chance. He waved to Vandy and saw the boy nod vigorously.

Nik sped for that end of the balcony, Vandy matching him. Below the boy dropped the blankets in a heap as Nik climbed over the balustrade. As he had hoped, that tangle cushioned his fall. Jarred but unhurt, he got to his feet.

"Which way do we go now?"

Vandy's question was apt. Nik could see no difference in the radiating tunnels, no difference save direction. In that way, they should reach toward the outer world and the place where the LB had set down, which meant toward the spot where Leeds should come, in turn. But wouldn't Orkhad reason the same way? Nik hesitated as he faced the dark mouths in what seemed the right direction—left, middle, right— If the Veep did hunt in that direction, he would have to split his force in three. Success might depend upon how many men he commanded. Nik made his decision and took the tunnel to the right.

"That way!"

Blaster in hand, he started down the track to discover that, once into the passage, they did not need the goggles after all. At well-spaced intervals, there were plates set in the walls that glowed dully. Nik thought that those who had built these ways had certainly not shared his type of eyesight—perhaps to that forgotten and doomed race, those plates had presented a maximum of light. Had Dis always been a night world for Terran stock or had the sun flare altered more than its surface?

"Where are we going now?" Vandy asked.

"Wherever we can hide until Captain Leeds comes."

"Who is he, Hacon, a Patrolman?"

Nik grinned wryly. Strode Leeds was probably far from a Patrolman, but he was certainly their only hope of surviving this venture.

"No—he's just the man who'll take us away from here." And Nik hoped that was the truth.

"When is he coming?"

When—that was the question! For the first in what might have been hours, Nik's left hand sought his face. Time—time to keep him what he now was or just to keep him and Vandy alive. The conflicting stories concerning the boy returned to plague Nik as they walked on along what seemed endless miles of tunnel, with no change in the walls, no sign there was any end to this burrow hollowed for an unknown purpose long before either of them had been born.

"I don't know." Nik roused to answer that last question.

"If we hide, how can we tell when he does come?" Vandy was practical.

"We'll have to find a hiding place from which we can see the landing apron," Nik replied. "Only near there is where they will hunt us, too."

"Go outside?" Vandy sounded doubtful, and Nik did not blame him.

Stay in the burrows where Orkhad could eventually track them down—go outside into a nightmare world where only a pair of goggles would give them freedom of movement, perhaps mean the difference between life and death? But also—to go outside was the only way to be sure of Leeds' arrival. Nik had no assurance of the wisdom of his own decisions. He could only make them by choosing the lesser of two evils. And he clung stubbornly to the idea that in Leeds lay their only safety now.

"Yes." His reply was curt. And then he began to wonder if they *could* reach the outside world—if this tunnel had any opening onto the surface of Dis.

"Look!" Vandy's outheld hand was a vague blur in the gloom. What he indicated lay mid-point between two of the dim lights. It was a greenish glow, stronger toward the roof, tapering as it descended. Nik pulled up the goggles, startled by the sharp focus that leaped at him.

Plants—or rather fleshy growths against the bare rock. They had no leaves Nik could identify but innumerable thin arms or branches that matted together, intertwining and twisting until they made a thick mass. And they grew through a break in the wall only a little below the room. A way outside?

Nik could not bring himself to touch that mat of weird vegetation with his bare hands. The stuff had such an unhealthy, even evil, look that he thought of poison or fungoid contamination. Yet the chance of an unexpected bolt hole could not be missed.

"What is it?" Vandy demanded, and Nik realized that to the boy's unaided eyes the growth was a hazy mystery.

"Maybe a side door if we can open it." Nik dialed the low beam on the blaster and turned it on that twisted mass.

There was a burst of flame licking across the whole growth in one consuming puff. The stench of that burning blew back at them, forcing a retreat. Then it was gone, and only stained rock remained. But the

66

crack the plants had masked was open, and there was light from it, light well visible to Nik's goggled eyes. Since the cleared space was big enough to scramble through, he leaped and caught at the sides, pulling himself up for a look.

Around him the concentrated stench made him gasp, and there was a whirl of thick and heavy smoke. It would seem that the fire started in the tunnel had ignited the vegetation here also.

Nik, coughing, held to his vantage point long enough to discover that the break was at the bottom of a wedgelike cut, the lips of which were far above. The fire puffed now up the walls of the cut, running with lightning speed along the trails of plants that must have originally choked most of that space.

The walls looked climbable, and Nik thought they had found their way out. He dropped back to wait for the fire to clear the cut, taking advantage of that interval to share a tin of rations with Vandy. They had food; now they must find a place to hole up for rest. Vandy had made no complaint, but Nik judged by his own growing fatigue that to climb out of the cut might be all the youngster could do.

He was right, Nik discovered, when they did climb. Vandy was slow, fumbling, and Nik used his belt as a safety device to link them. Vandy was not just tired; he was climbing that grade blind, making it necessary for Nik to guide his hands and feet. When they at last pulled out on top, Vandy sat panting, his head bowed on his knees.

"I—I don't think I can go on, Hacon—" he said in a small voice. "My legs—they're too shaky—"

Nik stood surveying the landscape about them with concentrated study. The ground was rough with many outcrops of rock among which grew lumpy plants, some inches high, others branching into the height of normal trees, but none of them wholesome-looking. The dank humidity of the outer world was a stifling blanket, weighing down their bodies almost as heavily as the fatigue. No, neither of them could go far now, and the rocks offered the best hope of shelter.

The nearest was a cluster of squared blocks where patches of growth made lumpy excrescences. Whether those rises also contained any protecting crevices or niches he could not be sure, but he was certain Vandy could not go much farther. Somehow, Nik got the boy to his feet and half led, half supported him to the rocks. The cloying scents in the air made them both gasp. And once or twice during that journey Nik gagged at a smell alien enough to human nostrils to arouse nausea.

A creature humped of spine, which moved by hops, broke from hiding almost under Nik's feet and took a soaring leap to the top of one of the blocks. There it slewed around. A tongue issued from a wide, gaping mouth to lash across a patch of fungi-encrusted stone and transfer a burden of harvested vegetation to that lipless stretch of warty skin.

Nik sighted the shadowy space beneath that hopping thing's perch. A moment later he supported Vandy to the edge of a dark pocket, pausing only to use the blaster to clear its interior. Then they were in a slit passage running on between the blocks. Nik pushed Vandy along that narrow way. It was not a cave. The continued regularity of the walls made him sure that this was the remains of a structure.

A rattle underfoot drew Nik's attention from the wall to the floor. He had kicked a grayish object. About as long as his forearm, it was formed of a series of rounded knobs linked together until his foot had disturbed them and several had rolled apart. Bones? Remains of what—and how recent the death that had left them there? Was this the lair of one of the killers of Dis?

Still, the way before them was open, and Nik had the blaster. Now he saw light ahead—further proof that this was a passage rather than a cave. Three or four more strides and he was fronted by an opening well above the surface of the way, a window to look out upon an eerie landscape so dark that even the goggles did not help much in his inspection.

Ruins—that was surely true. The block piles were regular in pattern. And they extended all along a shelf to his right. On the left was an abrupt drop, and then another, as if he were on the edge of a flight of steps intended for the use of giants.

No use trying to go on now, stumbling into the ruins. The window opening was well above the surface of the pavement, and if they bedded down immediately beneath it, they would be well protected. Nik was shaking with fatigue, and Vandy had slid out of his hold to lie still, his eyes closed, his panting breath coming in a more even pattern. Vandy was finished for now, and Nik had no strength to carry him. This had to be their refuge. He managed to spread the blankets and roll the boy on them. Then he sat down, his back against the wall, the blaster resting on his knee, wondering how long he could hold out against the sleep his body demanded.

7

Nik awoke to darkness, a black so thick it was a match for the humid air about him. He was choking, gasping, blinded. For those few seconds, panic held him, and then he remembered where he was. But before he could move, there was an awesome roll of sound, and he thought he could detect an answer of vibration through the stone pavement on which he crouched.

"Hacon—Hacon!" The appeal was half scream.

Nik flung out an arm, but Vandy was not there. He pawed at his chest, hunting the goggles that had rested there when he had nodded off into slumber. They too were missing! Vandy and the goggles. Had the boy tried to return to the LB?

"Hacon!" The call came from not too far away. Nik clawed up to the window facing the ruins. A thunderous roll shook the air and the earth under him. As it dwindled into silence, Nik heard other sounds, a growl, then a high-pitched scream. He clung to the edge of the window and tried to force sight where his eyes stubbornly refused to grant it.

"Vandy!" He put all his power into that shout. "Vandy!"

If there was an answer, the third peal of giant thunder swallowed it. A flash of dim radiance around the bowl of the horizon followed, while wind battered the scattered blocks. A storm was coming, and such a storm as was possible only on this nightmare world!

Nik tried to remember how the stretch beyond had looked when he had worn the goggles. There had been a relatively open space—he was sure of that—before the next ruined structure.

"Vandy!" Against hope, he bellowed again.

Then there was a flare, blinding in intensity, that started a column of flame Nik could use as a beacon. Vandy must have fired his blaster at some of the highly combustible native vegetation. With that as his guide, Nik began to run.

The wind caught at the ragged banners of the flames, tearing them into long, tattered ribbons, which ignited other growth beyond. Vandy—caught in that! A roar that was not thunder, but from some animal, sounded. Nik raced around broken column, a section of wall, and came into an arena where the fire lighted a wild scene.

Vandy was there, standing on a block of masonry, his back to a pillar or stele. And he held the blaster at ready, though he was not firing at what moved below.

Nik saw them clearly in the light of the fire, but how could you describe them? Each world having life on its surface had grotesques, things of beauty, things of horror, and how one classified them all depended upon one's own native range of comparison. These had beauty of a sort. Their elongated, furred bodies moved fluidly, wound in and out as if they were engaged in some formal dance. And their heads, with the double fur-fringed ears and the glowing eyes were raised and lowered in a kind of rhythm.

"Vandy," Nik shouted from instinct alone. "Don't watch them!"

Weaving patterns were produced by those lustrous fur bodies to draw the eyes and focus the attention. Nik looked above and behind the boy. His own blaster came up, its sights centered on twin pinpricks of light over Vandy's right shoulder. Nik fired. He had dialed the ray to needle beam, but even then he had had to aim high for fear of touching Vandy. That ray must have missed the attacker or attackers leading the sortie from above, but the eye gleams vanished, and the weaving pattern on the pavement ceased abruptly. The heads swung in Nik's direction as they stood still, eying him.

Here in the hollow among the ruins, the wind did not reach, but the fire had already eaten away at the growth and was now dying, so that Nik's sight of the hunters was curtailed. Several of the flankers dropped low, their belly fur brushing the ground as they glided toward him, pausing at once when he looked directly at them. They were not large animals. The biggest in the pack was as long as Nik's arm, but size did not mean too much if they hunted as a unit, and Nik thought that they did.

He began his circling, moving with his face toward the enemy, hoping to reach the point directly beneath Vandy's present perch. It was apparent that the creatures were cautious hunters. Perhaps somehow they had made a quick appraisal of the intruders' weapons in Vandy's use of the blaster.

Thunder was answered by a wide flash of the semi-invisible lightning. Neither sound nor light appeared to make any impression on the hunters. Nik had reached the edge of the stele; two more short steps would bring him below Vandy.

"Vandy!" He dared to hail the boy, and oddly enough his voice stopped the forward glide of the flankers and brought their heads up, swinging slightly from side to side as if the human mouthed word was far more disturbing than the approaching fury of the storm. "The goggles—" Nik held up his left hand without daring to see if the boy would obey him. "Give them here!"

A moment later the strap holding those precious windows into the dark was in his grasp. Then he heard Vandy.

"I'm covering—"

With that assurance, Nik dared to put the cin strap about his head and take the chance of looking away from the hunters. He gave a half whistle of relief. To have sight again—that was better than a glimpse or two with the aid of the almost dead fire. His confidence rose.

"Vandy"—he gave his orders slowly—"I'm going to move out from this block. You slide down behind me and take a grip on my tunic—now!"

Whatever influence his voice had had in the beginning on the pack was now wearing off. They had made a half circle about him, but so far they had not advanced beyond an invisible line of their own choosing.

He could not hear the sounds of Vandy's descent, for the thunder rolled deafeningly. A jerk on his tunic told him the boy had followed orders. Nik began to edge sideways, pulling Vandy with him, his body between the hunters and the boy, his blaster ready for the first sign of attack. Why the Disian creatures had not already pulled him down, Nik could not imagine. He reached the end of the block, and the full force of the storm-driven wind struck at him, bringing with it torrential rain.

Instantly the hunting pack vanished, leaving Nik to blink unbelievingly as he threw out his left arm and clawed for anchorage against the buffeting of wind and rain. It was as if they had simply disappeared into the slanting lines of the falling water itself!

Shelter— Nik did not think they could make it back to the window corridor across the open space where the storm hit with hammering strength. A flash—and through the cin-goggles the brilliance of the dark world's lightning was blinding. That must have hit close by.

Nik was aware of Vandy's pulling at him, urging him to the right. He looked over his shoulder. The boy had kept his hold on Nik with one hand; the fingers of the other had fastened in the edge of an opening between two blocks.

To venture into such a hideout might be walking into one of the hunters' dens, but they could not remain in the open. Already the force of the wind was driving through the air pieces of vegetation and other debris. There was one precaution he could take. Nik threw an arm about Vandy, holding him well anchored against his own body as he beamed the blaster into the opening. Then he stooped to enter.

Here even the cin-goggles were not much use. The pavement sloped down and inward from the door, and small rivers of rain poured about their boots. Nik halted. No use going on to a basin where the storm waters might gather. He could see walls faintly, near to hand at his right, farther away on his left. And there was a ledge or projection on the right.

"Ledge here." He guided Vandy's hand to that and swept the boy's palm back and forth across the slimed stone. "We'll stay there; too much water running down here."

Nik boosted the boy onto the projection and then settled beside him. The water was now flooding down the ramp. It was hard to believe it was merely storm overflow and not some stream diverted into this path. How far down did it run?

Even though sounds were muffled here, the fury of wind and rain and the assaults of thunder and lightning made a grumble that vibrated through the wall against which they huddled. Vandy's body pressed closer to Nik's with every boom from the outer world, and Nik kept his arm about the small shoulders, feeling the shudders that racked the boy's frame.

"Just a storm, Vandy." Nik sought to reassure the other.

But on Dis a storm might well be catastrophe of the worst kind. If he only knew more about this black world, about the Guild refuge and those in it, about Leeds—

For that matter, about Vandy, too. Why had the boy taken the goggles and gone into the ruins on his own? If he tried that trick again, it could well lead to disaster for both of them. Nik must make Vandy understand that.

"Why did you take the cins and go out?" Nik raised his voice above the gurgle of the rushing water, the more distant wind and rain, to ask.

Vandy squirmed in his hold. "I wanted to see if I could find the ship." His voice had a sullen note.

So, he had been heading for the LB.

"Vandy, I'm telling you the truth." Nik spoke slowly, trying to throw into his words every accent of conviction. "Even if we were right in the LB now, we couldn't rise off-world. It's locked on a homing device to this port, and I can't reset that."

There was no answer from the other save that his body stiffened in Nik's hold as if he would pull away. Nik kept his grip tight.

Vandy was still stiff in his hold when he spoke. His lips were so close to Nik's ear that the puffs of his breath touched the other's now smooth cheek.

"There's something—something on the ledge—over there!"

Nik turned his head slowly. It was almost totally dark for him even with the goggles. How *could* Vandy see anything? A ruse to distract him? It *was* there, and to Nik's eyes it showed with frightening plainness. Where had it come from—out of the watery depths below or down the wall from above? Its hunched body had some of the greenish glow of the crushed slime plants, but Nik could not be sure of more than a phosphorescent lump.

Between them and it dangled a glowing spark that danced and fluttered. It took a full moment for Nik to trace that spark back to the humped body to which it was attached by a slender, whip-supple antenna. Now another of those antenna snapped up into action, and a second spark glistened at its tip, flickering about. Save for that play, the thing made no move to advance toward them.

But before that display of twin dancing lights, there was other movement on the ledge. Whether the second creature had been there all the time or whether the action of the antenna fisher had drawn it, Nik was never to know. But a four-legged furred shape, like one of the hunters, arose from a flattened position and began to pace hesitatingly toward the fisher.

The antennae with their flashing tips slowly withdrew, luring the other after them. The pacer showed no excitement nor wariness; it followed the lures unresistingly.

"What—what is happening?" whispered Vandy, and Nik realized that the goggles gave him a view of the hunt that the boy lacked.

"Something is hunting." He described what he saw.

The drama ended suddenly. As the antennae vanished into the owner's bulk, the prey appeared to awake to its danger. But already the fisher had launched itself from the stone with a flying leap into the air that brought it down on the unfortunate it had lured into striking distance. There was a shrill humming either from fisher or prey, and Vandy cried out, his hands catching Nik's tunic.

Continuing to crouch on its captive, the fisher was still. Nik could not yet sight a separate head—nothing save a bulk with that unhealthy, decaying sheen about it.

"Hacon, it wants—it wants us!" Vandy did not whisper now. His voice was shrill. Whether that was a guess on his part or whether some sense of malice was transmitted to the boy, Nik did not know. But when those twin twinkling, dangling lights once more erupted from the black bulk and whipped through the air in their direction, he chose prudence and used the blaster.

As the ray lanced into the bulk, Nik caught his breath. He was not sure that he actually heard anything. It was more like a pain thrusting into his head than any cry his ears reported. But the thing and its prey twisted up and fell down into the rush of waters, to be carried on into whatever depths the ancient ruins covered.

"It's gone!" he assured Vandy. "I rayed it—it's gone!"

Vandy's shivers were almost convulsive, and Nik's alarm grew. He must get the boy under control, arouse him from the fear that made his body starkly rigid in Nik's hold—that had frozen him.

"It's gone!" he repeated helplessly. But he knew

what might lie at the base of Vandy's terror. To be blind in this hole could feed any fear, could drive even a grown man to panic. If they only had two sets of goggles! And what if something happened to the one pair they did possess? What if both of them were left wandering blind on the outer shell of Dis, prey for the creatures of the dark? Their flight from the refuge had been a wild mistake. He was armed now. Better go back and take his chances with Orkhad than remain in this wilderness of horror.

Just let the storm die and they would do that. Nik could find the trail back from this point to the break in the tunnel, and from the tunnel he could scout the living quarters of the refuge, find a safe hiding place until Leeds came—

"Vandy!" He strove to make his words penetrate the locked terror he could feel in the body he held. "We're going back to the tunnel just as soon as the rain is over. We'll be safe there. And until then—well, we both have blasters. You used yours, remember, when the animals had you cornered in the ruins. Used it well, too. I couldn't have found you if you hadn't set fire to the plants. We hold this ledge. Nothing can come at us here as long as we're armed."

"But—I can't *see!*"

"Are you sure, Vandy? You told me that thing was there before I saw it, and I have the goggles. How *did* you know?"

Vandy's body was not quite so rigid and his voice, when he replied, was alive again and not dehumanized with terror. "I guess I saw something—a sort of pale light—like those plants we squashed with our boots."

"Yes. Some of the living things here appear to have a light of their own. And maybe you could see that better than I could just because you did *not* have goggles on, Vandy. Perhaps we'll need both kinds of sight to watch here." How true that guess might be Nik did not know, but its effect on the boy was good.

"Yes." Vandy loosed one hand hold. "And I do have the other blaster."

"Don't use it unless you have to," Nik was quick to warn. "I don't know how long a charge will last."

"I know that much!" Vandy had recovered to the point of being irritated. "Hacon, this was all part of a city once, wasn't it? It's scary though—like the Haperdi Deeps—"

If Vandy could return to one of his fantasy adventures for a comparison, Nik decided, he was coming out of his fright.

"Yes, it was a city, I think. And it does seem like the Haperdi Deeps, though I don't recall that we ran into any fishers with light for bait there." He hoped Vandy's confidence would not soar again to the point of confusing reality with fantasy, regaining a belief in their own invincibility. Hacon, the hero, could wade through battles with horrific beasts and aliens untouched, but Nik Kolherne was very human and perishable, as was Vandy, and the hope of survival must move them both. He said as much, ending with a warning as to what might happen if the cin-goggles suffered any damage before they regained the refuge. To his satisfaction, Vandy was impressed.

Now that he had made his decision to return, Nik was impatient to be on his way, but the water still rushed down beyond the ledge. And now and then the roll of thunder, the cry of the storm, carried to them. How long would this fury of Disian weather last? A day—or longer? And could they remain on their present perch for any length of time? Nik had no fear that they could not defend it against attack, but fatigue and hunger could be worse enemies. The supply containers they had brought with them had been left with the blankets back in the window passage. Already Nik was hungry and knew that Vandy must be also.

Time dragged on. Vandy went to sleep, his head resting on Nik's knees. Now and then he gave a little whimper or said a word or two in a tongue that was not the basic speech of the galaxy. Nik had plenty of opportunity to plan ahead, to examine all that had happened. He would, he decided, have done the same again—given his word to Leeds and the Guild for a new face. And the payment was bringing Vandy to Dis. Bringing Vandy—

Leeds' story of what was wanted from the boy and Orkhad's counter story— Vandy believed his father still alive. *Did* Vandy have information the Guild wanted, or was the boy himself the goods they were prepared to deal in?

Nik's fingers slipped back and forth across smooth cheek and chin, across flesh that felt firm and healthy, bone that was hard and well-shaped. How long would he continue to feel that? How long before his fingertips detected new, yet well-remembered, roughness there to signal his own defeat? There was no possible answer except to wait for Leeds.

And to tamp that thought and the uneasiness behind it well back into his mind, Nik tried to assess his immediate surroundings. They had not come too far from the tunnel opening. They could get back, and most of the way was under cover. His ears gave him hope. The rush of water below had slackened, and he did not hear the wild sounds of the storm any more. Even a lull would allow them to regain the window passage and the food there. He shook Vandy gently.

"Time to go—"

8

Nik tested the current of the flood on the downward slope by lowering himself to stand with it washing about his boots while he held to the ledge. The water was glassy; its dark surface rippled now and then. Sometimes those ripples ran against the current as if life fought a passage upward. But the wash came no higher than Nik's ankles, and the force of it was not enough to impede wading.

At his assurance, Vandy dropped down, keeping a hold on Nik as he had when they had faced the hunters. Then they splashed toward the outside.

There it was still raining steadily, but the wildness of the wind had abated. The rain flowed by every depression to the edge of the drop the ruins lined, cascading over in countless small falls. There was something about that abrupt drop—could this city once have been a port on a long-vanished river or sea? But the mystery of the ruins was not their problem. To get back to the tunnel was.

"Keep hold," Nik ordered Vandy as he pushed into the open under the pelt of the rain.

Now—that *was* the window through which he had climbed! He boosted Vandy up and scrambled after. They were in the dry again, and Nik looked for the supplies. He triggered the heat-and-open button on one of the containers, holding it with care lest some of the precious contents spill. When the lid sprang up and the steam made his mouth water, he gave it to Vandy.

"Eat it all, but slowly," Nik ordered and took up

another tin for himself. Rationing might be more sensible, but it had been a long time since their last meal. Nik felt they needed full stomachs for the job ahead. Once back in the refuge, there would be chances to get more supplies.

The humidity, which had been so choking before the storm, seemed even worse in the narrow passage. The smallest effort left Nik gasping. His clothes, soaked in the rain, had no chance of drying, but he made Vandy strip and wipe down with one of the blankets, doing the same himself, before huddling into their soggy clothes once more.

"My boots—they're shining," Vandy observed suddenly.

Nik glanced down. There was an odd luminescence outlining the boy's footgear—his own, too. He examined them more closely. A furred substance was there. Nik had a dislike of investigating by finger touch. With a blanket edge he wiped Vandy's boot toe. There was a slimy feel to the smear, and the blanket came away phosphorescent as had their tracks upon first entrance to the refuge. Their boots were growing some form of vegetation!

Quickly Nik surveyed the rest of their clothing. His belt—yes, that had the same warning glow, and so had parts of the ornamental harness Vandy had dreamed up for Hacon's uniform. But, save for the boots, Vandy appeared free. Neither of them dared to discard those boots and venture bare-skinned across Disian earth. Whether they were now carrying some deadly danger with them, Nik did not know. He could only hope that the weird growth would not root on their skins.

There had been vegetation in the tunnel, but where the roof break had admitted it, and it had not spread far from that point. Perhaps the cool current of air always flowing through the refuge was a discouraging factor. All the more reason for getting back there.

With their remaining supplies repacked, Nik steered Vandy down the passage. They had reached the other door of that way and were near to the cut where the tunnel entrance lay when Vandy cried out. But Nik saw it, too, and there was no mistaking that kind of fire. A small ship was riding tail flames down for a landing, probably on the same field where the LB had finned in. That must be Leeds!

"There's another!" Vandy cried. "And—"

Two ships—a third! Leeds couldn't be leading a fleet! Was Vandy right? Were those his father's ships, a father who was not dead but lured here with Vandy for the bait? But if that was true, where did Leeds stand? Nik halted the run that had brought him to the edge of the cut.

The rain was pouring into the bottom of that hollow. It must be curling in turn into the tunnel. Their back door might not even be practical—if they still wanted to use it. That *if* was important, and its answer could only come by learning the identity of the planeting ships.

There was noise—not one of the great thunderclaps of the Disian storm, but a shock through the ground under them. Vandy screamed and tumbled forward into the cut. Nik tried to grasp him. One hand caught a hold, and then the two of them were sliding down. Nik brought up against a rock with painful force, but that anchored them against a farther tumble. There was a second shock in the ground, and out of the tunnel break air exploded, carrying with it bits of rock and soil.

Down in the refuge, there had been an explosion. Had Orkhad taken some drug-twisted way out of trouble by blowing up his own stronghold? Or had the refuge been forced from without and was it now under attack? At any rate, to drop into those depths at present was asking for worse trouble than they had faced so far.

"Got—to—get—away—" Nik panted. "Whole thing might collapse under us here—"

One of his arms and one side were pinned to the ground by Vandy's weight and the boy had neither spoken nor moved since they had landed there.

"Vandy!" Nik edged his head around.

Closed eyes, a trickle of blood across the forehead—Vandy must be unconscious. Nik strove to wriggle free. His movements brought an answering throb of pain. That slam against the rock had not been the easiest landing in the world. But Vandy, the boy might be seriously injured—

Their anchoring rock had seemed to give a little when Nik moved. He began to claw at the soil under him, loosening enough so that he could squirm around and put his head and shoulders upslope. The trails of rain were still flooding down. Splashes from one struck them. Vandy moaned and tried to move, but Nik was quick to pin him down. Another wriggle and they both might be on their way to the bottom. Luckily, there had been no more quakes or explosions or whatever had stirred up the earth hereabouts.

With Vandy a dead weight, Nik was defeated when it came to climbing, and he feared to descend. That explosion of air and rock must have blown a larger hole in the tunnel. To fall into whatever might be in progress down there was more danger than he cared to face.

A sidewise progress upslope—yes, he could make that—but not carrying Vandy. Could he leave the boy there, wedged in behind the rock, while he went to the top and devised some method of raising Vandy in turn? The boy was half conscious now but not alert enough to understand their predicament and cooperate by remaining quiet. Left, he could well fall into the tunnel hole.

The wet slope was a slippery way at best, but Nik still had the small pack of blankets and supplies. The blankets themselves? Nik tried to think coherently and purposefully.

He moved with infinite caution, dragging Vandy across his thighs so that the boy lay face up behind the rock. Then Nik unfastened the blanket roll and pulled it around.

Somehow, he managed the next move. One of the blankets was wrapped around Vandy, confining his arms and legs, the belt made fast, and the other blanket used again as a rope. From this point, the climb seemed mountain high, but Nik knew from their first journey out of the cut that it was not. If he could make the effort, they would win.

He chose to tackle the slope between two water streams where the earth was relatively dry, if any stretch of ground on this bedeviled world could be deemed that. Now he straightened cautiously and drove two of the supply containers into the yielding surface with all the strength he could muster, hanging his weight on each as a test.

Anchorage for a gain, now use the last two above those! Nik crawled face down against the slimed earth. It was time to loosen the lower containers—but only one would come free as he leaned at an almost impossible angle to struggle with it. Well, that one would have to serve. Drive it in above—crawl—

Then his clawing hand was over the edge where a portion of the cut wall had earlier collapsed. Nik strained with the effort to rise and rolled over into a puddle of rain.

He heard a moan from below and edged around. His arms were like heavy weights. Nik was not really certain that his overtaxed muscles would obey his demand for more effort. His breathing came in snorts, which did not supply enough air to his laboring lungs, but he grasped the end of the blanket rope and began to pull.

The package that was Vandy slipped around, and for once the slick ground surface served rather than thwarted. Nik pulled with a desperate need for getting this over and brought Vandy upslope into the same puddle where he knelt.

Now, only a few feet and they would be at the top. Nik did not have enough energy left to lift Vandy. Pushing the boy before him, he crept up the incline and lay there, the humid air thick in his nostrils, seeping with difficulty into his lungs.

It was then that the third and last shock came. For one desperate instant, Nik thought they would slide back. He flung out an arm to roll Vandy on and kicked himself away from the slipping earth. So they were saved from being carried down once more.

As soon as that upheaval ended, Nik began to crawl, pulling Vandy, determined to get away from the danger point, not really caring in which direction, so long as it was not down. They were in the open among the ruins, and the sheets of rain continued to sweep over and about them.

Nik headed for the passage from which they had emerged only a short time earlier, desiring nothing now but to be out of that torrent. He was almost under that cover when he heard, above the rain, a sharp crack that he could not believe was part of the natural noise of the storm. He hunched around, his hand to his blaster.

Out and up from somewhere near the landing field it soared, not one of the winged Disian creatures but a flier—and a planet atmosphere craft, not a spacer.

It skimmed through the rain like a black shadow, seeking no great altitude, rising only far enough to clear the heights that roofed the refuge. Then it headed out across the ruins of the ancient city.

Tracers of fire followed that flight, shooting angry lashings into the storm. Nik was not familiar with the tricks of evasive action, but he sensed that the unknown pilot was making a masterly escape from whatever fate had overtaken one party or the other in the storming of the refuge. That the fleeing man or men in the flitter were of the Guild he had little doubt which meant that the invaders were in control below and on the landing strip.

But who were the invaders? Forces of Vandy's people? Leeds' men forcing a showdown with Orkhad—though Nik hardly believed that. Could Leeds have mustered three ships, which he estimated had been used to break into the refuge? Law in the persons of the Patrol?

He crouched there, watching the shadow of the flitter weaving back and forth, flying low in the rain. At least the invaders were firing only ground-based missiles, not making chase by air.

There was a splash of fire to the right. One of the missiles had fouled with a fire ray and exploded with a clap of sound. Then one of those fire spears touched a fin wing on the flitter. The craft whirled, fluttering back and forth. Nik tensed, imagining the frantic fight of the pilot to keep the machine aloft or sufficiently under control to land it safely.

The flitter sideslipped to Nik's left. It was falling rather than landing under control. But before it was quite out of sight, it steadied. If it did make a landing, it would be down in the gulf of the drop below the ruined city, perhaps on the bed of what seemed a one-time sea.

And those who had aimed the lucky shot that finished it—they would be moving out to hunt the wreckage, which meant they would come in this direction! Nik chewed on that unhappy reflection. If he remained where he was, he would be detected. If this was the Patrol or any official expedition hunting Vandy, they would be equipped with any number of devices to locate another human on Dis. He had heard a lot of stories about such mechanical man-hunters. And to be scooped up now by either party would mean his own death warrant, as he well knew. The squadron that had used such force to break into the refuge would not be tempted to argue out a surrender. Nor could he be sure they were on the law's side.

Orkhad had hinted at two parties in the Guild. This could be a jack job. If he only knew!

What Nik did know, however, was that this was not a good place to stay.

"Hacon—" Vandy wriggled in the blanket roll, striving to throw off his bindings. "What—what happened?"

"A lot." Nik knew a small surge of relief. If Vandy was conscious and able to go on his own two feet, their flight would be easier.

And flight it was going to have to be! There was a smoldering, sputtering patch of fire on the heights where a ray had ignited vegetation. The highly inflammable stuff seemed able to burn even in the rain, and the smog of that burning carried through the thick air as a stifling gas.

Nik pulled the wrappings from Vandy as they both choked and coughed. To return to the ruins would do no good. Not only were there the things that lived in the shadows there, but also the gas of the burning settled thickest in that direction. They should get down to a lower level. And that would take them in the general direction of the vanished flitter, along the very path pursuit would come, but they were cut off on the other three sides.

Nik leaned over Vandy. "Can you walk?" He asked the immediate question.

"I think so—"

He hoped that was the truth. But when he helped the boy to his feet, Nik kept his arm about those small shoulders. Then, half guiding, half supporting Vandy, he started on through the ruins to hunt some way down the cliff the city edged. And, with Vandy lacking cin-goggles, Nik's sight had to do for them both.

Their first break of better fortune came when the rain actually began to slacken. That needling force of water was now a drizzle, and the streams finding their ways across the broken and earth-drifted pavement were thinning visibly. By the cin-fostered sight, it was now as light as cloud-gloomed Korwarian day, and Nik was thankful for that.

They threaded a path along the verge of the cliff, and Nik sighted piles of tumbled blocks that might once have been wharfs for the convenience of surface shipping. One of those they used as a stairway down to the first level below the city surface, where the oily vapors of the burning had not reached.

Nik's throat was raw with coughing, and Vandy was sobbing as they came to the end of that tough scramble. There was a large pool there filling a depression but already draining through a channel toward the outer reaches of the onetime sea. Nik went down on one knee beside it and put his hand into the liquid.

So far they had managed on the supplies from the refuge, but those were gone. Now they would have to chance the water and what food they could find on Dis, and that chance would be only one more danger in the many they faced.

Nik scooped up a palmful of the water. It had no scent he could detect. And they had inadvertently swallowed some of it in the form of rain on their lips and faces ever since they had been caught in the first gusts of the storm. He licked up some of the moisture greedily, and it relieved the parching of his mouth and throat.

"Water, Vandy!" Nik cupped his hands and filled them, lifting the trickling burden to the boy's lips and supplying more a second and third time.

How long this water would last, Nik could not tell, but it was now a wealth all about them. And their path at present would take them along the foot of the old shoreline cliff, away from the refuge. What their goal was, Nik could not have said, except shelter of some kind until he might gain some idea of the forces now ranged against them. How he was going to make that identification without walking directly into the enemies' hands, he had no knowledge, either.

The same fungoid vegetation that grew thickly above straggled here, but not in such profusion or size. Nik avoided the patches whenever he could, remembering how their boots had left trails of shining prints before. The rain was coming to an end, and the measure of daylight increased. It was hard for him to recall that this was still black night for Vandy. He kept reminding himself of that fact, keeping his hand on the boy's shoulder as a guide.

Vandy was not going to be able to keep up this travel for very much longer. Nik could carry him for a while, and he would, but there would be a limit to that also. They must hole up somewhere for a rest, and yet, for all their efforts, they were still so close to the refuge, so easily tracked by any pursuers.

The ruins of the old wharves were well behind. When Nik looked up at the one-time shore, he saw that there had been an increase of height there, as if the ancient city had been walled on this side by small mountains. And the cliff to his right soared higher and higher. Its surface was broken by the dark, ragged patches of cave mouths. This once must have been a wild place when the sea battered along those walls. Ahead and not too far away, an arm of the cliff stretched out to bar their present path with a wall of rock, which must mark an old cape dwindling to a reef. And that was a barrier they could not pass in their present fatigue. Somewhere along the broken length of that Nik must find them a temporary refuge which he could turn into a fortress against pursuit.

9

Nik raised his head from his forearm. It was full day, and the steaming heat brought visible curls of vapor from the recently drenched soil until there was a mist lacing the rocks. Back in the shallow cave hole he guarded, Vandy was sleeping in a small measure of coolness. But how long could either of them continue to take the surface atmosphere of Dis?

Both their boots were covered with a red fur of growth, which appeared in patches also on Nik's belt and the ornamental tabs of his tunic. Even though they had washed in pools of rock-held rain water, they could not free their skins from a greasy feel, which carried the sensation of perpetual filthiness. And there was never any chance to be really dry! Clothing continued soggy and almost pulpy to the touch.

The mist was nearly as hindering to the vision as the loss of the cins might be, Nik thought dully. Anything or anyone might be creeping upon them now within its twisting, curling envelope. And he believed that his powers of hearing were also distorted.

So far, their occupancy of the barrier crevice had been challenged by only one creature—a thing of long, jointed legs, the first pair of which had been armed with claws of assorted sizes. Stalked eyes had sighted them and brought the thing scuttling in their direction, but a blaster beam had curled it up wriggling, to kick away its life at the foot of a nearby rock. And since its floppings had subsided, smaller things had cautiously ventured forth to sample a feast they had never expected to enjoy so opportunely.

Its attack had taught Nik the need for wariness. Only there was a limit to endurance, and he had reached it, nodding now into unquiet dozes from which he roused with a start of warning. He would soon have to wake Vandy, to trust the boy not only with a blaster but also with the cin-goggles when he went on sentry duty. And dared Nik do that? What had happened back in the ruins when Vandy had taken off on his own was still in Nik's mind. Had he made plain to the boy the danger of trying such a run? Luckily, Vandy had not shown any interest in the nature of the pursuit Nik expected. But suppose Vandy did believe that those were his father's men back at the refuge. Would he try to return?

Did he believe Nik's explanation of a fight among the men there—a rift in the Guild forces? Vandy had witnessed the landing of the spacers, which could have been the enemy. To place the boy on sentry-go was the same, or could be the same, as inviting him to desert.

However, if Nik waited until he went under from sheer exhaustion, then Vandy would have an easy opportunity to leave, which he might not be so inclined to do if his companion shared some of the responsibility with him. It all depended now on how much of the Hacon influence remained. Vandy had shown signs of breaking with his fantasy several times lately. On the other hand, he also clung to Nik, appealing for help and comfort. Would Nik remain Hacon if Vandy faced in their pursuers someone he knew or would he turn on Nik for what he was now, a kidnaper and an outlaw.

There were two choices, and his brain was too tired to make a clear-headed selection. Either way, Nik might be choosing his own end. But wearily he turned and reached to touch the sleeping boy's leg.

Moments later, blind in the eerie dark of non-goggle sight, Nik stretched out in the hollow between the rocks. He could not even be sure that Vandy was in the lookout, ready to obey orders and arouse Nik at the first sign of any native creature or off-world searchers. He sighed, unable to raise again his weighted eyelids. His last awareness was of the blaster, about the butt of which his fingers tightened.

Muddled dreams haunted him, of which he could remember only a sense of frustration and terror. He came out of them groggily at some urging he was not able to understand at once.

"Hacon!"

Nik sat up, obeying the pull at his shoulder, blinking into a dark broken here and there with feeble touches of a pallid luminescence. Vandy leaned above him.

"Over there!"

But "over there" was still a mystery in the dark for Nik, trying to assemble some measure of wits.

"I can't see—" he protested dully.

"Here!" The goggles came into his hand. He put them on and faced in the direction Vandy indicated.

It was disturbing to have sight return instantly with the aid of those lenses. The reef was clear, sharp as it would be under normal sunlight. Nik looked for what had excited the boy.

"Where—?" he began, and then he saw it! Or rather—them!

Issuing from a rock-bordered crevice well along the reef, fronting what must once have been the waters of the vanished sea, was a trio of creatures. They stood very still, heads aloft, as if facing into the wind and spray of the past. Nik brought up the blaster and sighted on the nearest of that trio, before he noted that there was no stir in their position, that no pull of breath moved their monstrous sides, that the wind did not disturb the thick manes that lay about their massive shoulders.

The watchers were not alive; yet the long-forgotten artist who had created them had given such a semblance of reality to their fashioning as to make deception easy.

In form, they were not unlike the creatures that had surrounded Vandy in the ruins save that they were much larger, majestic in their stance. The black of their bodies was stark against the lighter gray and red of the rocks, and Nik caught a glisten of eye in the one he had originally marked as a target, as if some glittering gem gave it the necessary touch of realism.

Guardians of the coast, symbolically erected to warn off invaders in times past, he wondered? Monument to some ancient feat or victory.

Then Nik started. There—there was something—someone behind the watchers!

A shadow of rock overhung that spot, so that his line of vision was obscured. But, he knew after a moment of study, he had been right—there was something behind the statues. And to see it clearly, he would have to leave their crevice refuge and work his way farther along the reef. He said as much to Vandy.

"But the animals—" the boy protested.

"They look alive, but they are just statues. It's what's behind them counts now—"

"I'm going, too," Vandy declared.

These rocks were nothing to cross without cins, but Nik could not order him to remain. He gave the goggles back for a time, made Vandy survey the stretch they must negotiate, and then resettled them over his own eyes. With Vandy linked by a hold on his belt, Nik began a creeping advance along the weathered reef.

Now, he should be able to see from here—unless the lurker had moved in turn. With caution, Nik braced one arm against a spire of stone and leaned well back to look up at the watchers.

He jerked up his blaster and then hesitated. Again the supreme art of the sculptor or sculptors had deceived his off-world eyes. There was something standing behind the watchers, yes, but it, too, was stone.

Nik blinked, almost gasped. Just seconds earlier there had been no head there! Now there was a black furred one, gazing from that point straight out over the drained sea bottom with much the same fixity of stare as the three giant watchers. But the static pose of that head did not remain. It changed position, turned on the green shoulders, and Nik knew that what he saw was one of the hunters from the ruins mounted on the broken figure as if on lookout duty.

A scout for the hunting pack? If so, this might be the most dangerous perch he and Vandy could have. To be caught among the broken rocks by those hunters could be disastrous. Did the creature hunt by sight or scent? And how many of its kind would follow it?

Nik flattened himself against the rock spire, whispered a warning to Vandy, and stared about him. Every shadowed crevice was now suspect. But, if they went out into the open sea bottom where there was no cover for the enemy, then he was sure he could hold off any rush by blaster fire. He remembered how the ambush had been set up in the ruins—those eyes that had betrayed the hunter creeping on Vandy from above. Yes, get out—get away from the rocks, which could cover an attack.

But to strike out into the sea bottom itself— As long as they kept the shoreline for a guide, they would not be lost to the general neighborhood of the refuge. Their supplies were gone. The rain pools could provide water, but they had to have food—and Nik had clung to the faint hope that there might be some chance of getting that from some dump at the Guild base. Yes, they could take to the open of the sea bottom but not out so far as to lose contact with the shore as a point of reference.

He glanced again at the figure behind the watchers. Once more the green shoulders were headless. And that fact drove him into action. With Vandy holding to his belt, guided by his instructions, they climbed over the reef and headed out toward the open, where the low growing vegetation could provide no cover for an attack.

Once off the skirts of the reef, the walking was easier, and they moved faster. Nik kept looking back to check their trail. A good view of the watchers and their headless companion could be had from this point, and he had been right about the eyes of the former—they flashed now and then as if they were

94

lighted within. But the shoulders of the green man were bare; the furred scout had not returned.

Luckily, much of the mist and steam that had drifted from the ground earlier had been diffused, and Nik judged the extent of visibility gave him a present advantage over any trailers—from Dis or from the refuge—always providing the latter were not airborne. He set a course that kept to the bottom land just a little to shoreward of that second sharp drop to another one-time sea level.

Below, the runnels of water had fed a lake of some size, though the streamlets themselves were dwindling fast, many leaving only cuts as reminders of their flood courses. And on that lower level the vegetation was even scantier. Hillocks of rock sprouted from the lake's surface, one such rising to a respectable height, and Nik guessed that its crown had once been a true island.

He did not stop his inspection of their back trail. And it was on the third such pause for careful survey that he thought he detected a hint of movement at the base of the reef, as if what lurked there was taking care not to be sighted. The pack on the hunt? Or even an off-world scout of his own species?

"Hacon, is there something to eat?" Vandy waited quietly, not losing his hold on Nik's belt. "I'm hungry."

Nik licked his own lips. The supply tins were back in the tunnel cut. What dared they use of Dis to answer the demands of their bodies for sustaining fuel? He gagged at the thought of attempting to mouth any of the growing stuff about them. Meat—one of those thin-legged, clawed creatures such as had stalked them on the reef? Or one of the furred hunters that might be trailing them? Or something such as that fisher in the dark of the ruins? When it was a choice between life and starvation, a man could stamp down repugnance born of appearance.

"We'll find something." He tried to make that reassuring and knew that he would have to fulfill that promise soon.

There was a screech torturing to his off-world ears.

Vandy cried out, his eyes straining to pierce the dim, but Nik saw clearly. Not so far ahead there was a commotion on the verge of the rain lake below. Winged things flapped and fought over a surface that was ruffled and dimpled in turn, as if some life form wallowed and swam. One of the fliers made a dive into the center of the disturbance and arose, uttering harsh squawks of what might have been triumph, since it carried in its claws writhing, scaled prey.

Two of the flier's fellows followed it aloft, harassing it as if to make it drop its capture, rather than trying a catch on their own. The successful hunter dodged, screamed, and skimmed just above the surface of the higher level, while its tormentors harried it with determination.

One soared and then made a sudden swoop, deadly intention in every beat of its sustaining leathery wings. The attacked made a futile effort to evade and crashed into the companion pursuer. There was a squawking, screeching whirl of fighting fliers falling fast to the ground. The prey the first had raped from the lake was loosed.

The airborne battle had swept close to the place where Nik and Vandy stood. And the twisting, turning captive fell only a little away. That third combatant, which had delivered the attack from above, avoided the struggling fighters that had also struck the ground and were still clawing at each other. It swooped above Nik as if some of its fury had been transferred to the man.

Almost in reflex action, he fired the blaster, catching the flier full on. The force of the ray blast carried the creature back so that it fell, already dead, over the cliff to the lake level. Then weapon still in hand, Nik strode forward to inspect the cause of battle.

It was still flopping feebly, but even as he came up, it straightened out and was still. Though its body was weirdly elongated, it bore some resemblance to a fish, enough so that Nik picked it up.

One of the battlers had left the other and came scuttling across the ground screeching, its long neck outstretched, its narrow head darting back and forth with a jerky vehemence. One wing was held at a queer angle, and there was blood smearing its torn body.

Nik jumped to the left, and the creature sped on, seemingly unable to change course—to plunge over the cliff like the flier before it.

"Hacon! Hacon, what was it? What are those things? What are they doing?" Vandy's voice was shrill. To him, the struggle must have been frightening, carried on in the dark.

Swiftly Nik explained. He was still holding the fish, and now he let Vandy examine it by touch.

"Is it good to eat, Hacon?"

"It could be." Nik hesitated. Anything put in their mouths on Dis might be rank poison, but they had to start somewhere, and perhaps that was here and now.

"How do we cook it?" Vandy continued.

"We don't," Nik replied shortly.

"Eat it—like this?" Vandy faltered. He almost dropped the limp body.

"If we have to, yes. But not here and now." Nik was hungry, and even the thought of eating a Disian fish raw did not diminish that hunger. But he had no intention of consuming it here, when they could be the focus of attack from other predators. He took the fish from Vandy and hooked it into one of his belt attachments, one that was free of any phosphoresence.

As they skirted the cliff, they saw other turmoil in the lake and witnessed the fishing of other fliers. The winged creatures appeared reluctant to touch water in taking their prey. Only a few dared that, as if the lake held some menace they feared.

The lake itself stretched along the second cliff edge, lapping the outcroppings of the irregular ground. The surface on which Vandy and Nik traveled was sloping down with indications of eventually merging with the lower level, while the cliffs of the one-time shore were rising.

Nik made another cast behind. And this time the pursuers were not so careful to keep concealed. A furred hunter stood over the flier killed in combat by its fellow. It nosed the body and then began to eat.

"Hurry—!" Nik caught at Vandy, pulling the boy along. Ahead he could see one of the island hillocks, though this must have been a mere dot of island in the days when the sea washed this land. The light was less than it had been when they had left the reef. Nik did not doubt that the day's end was coming. And at night that hillock might mean safety. Perched up there, they would have defense against anything that would climb to attack.

Another glance showed him that a second hunter had joined the first at the feast. Unlike the fliers, the first did not attempt to drive off or attack his fellow but moved a little to one side, allowing the newcomer a chance at the food. This was odd enough to make Nik wonder. Cooperation in feeding, as well as hunting, suggested a higher form of consciousness than the fliers, who tore each other for the prey. The hunters were smaller editions of those three magnificent watchers on the headland. They had been esteemed by the original natives of Dis to the point that infinite care had been taken to establish highly artistic representations of their species on a prominent place before the city. Animals that had been sacred to the one-time rulers of this world? Pets—protection?

"I can't go—so—fast—" Vandy stammered. He stumbled and nearly fell.

Nik, eaten by the need for some form of shelter before the coming of what was a double dark, caught him up and kept on. They were directly below the island hill. He struggled up and on, finally pulling out on an expanse of rock ledge below a sharp crest. He pushed Vandy back against that crest and looked back.

There were the furred hunters, still eating, and still only the two of them in sight. If they were scouts for a pack, the rest had not yet caught up. Now, Nik got to his feet and turned slowly to get a good look at what lay about them. To his right was the rain lake, to his left a dip and then the cliff of the old shore.

Anything trying to reach their present perch must either swim the lake and then wind up an almost sheer drop or come up the same way he and Vandy had used, to be met by blaster fire. They had their refuge for the night, as safe a one as he could devise.

Nik sat down and unhooked the fish from his belt. Methodically, he cleaned it and cut the whole into portions. They would now try the provender of Dis.

10

"Vandy! Vandy!"

Nik held the boy, wondering whether that violent retching would ever stop, whether the convulsions that shook the small body could be endured for long, his feeling of guilt rising like an answering sickness within him. He had never witnessed such a terrible attack of nausea before. It was as if the few bites of fish Vandy had taken had been virulent poison; yet they had had no similar effect on Nik.

Vandy lay limp now, moaning a little, and Nik hesitated. Should he try to get him to drink some water or would that bring on another attack? He feared another such violent upheaval might be truly dangerous. There was nothing he *could* do for Vandy—no medicine he could offer. Back at the refuge—

Back at the refuge—to return there— If Vandy's people had led the attack, or the Patrol— But suppose the other possibility was the truth, that the struggle had been some inter-Guild dispute? Or was Nik clinging to that merely because it was what he wanted to believe for his own safety? Vandy's head rolled on Nik's shoulder; the boy's breathing was heavy, labored.

In spite of the night, with the cin-goggles, he could start now, carry Vandy, retrace their journey, and find the hunters waiting out there while he was too burdened with the boy to make a fighting stand. Nik bit his lip and tried to think clearly. This could be only a passing illness for Vandy; the boy could have an allergy to the strange food. And to be caught by the hunters—

Perhaps to wait right here until any trailers from the refuge came would be the wise move. Nik could remain with Vandy until he saw them coming, then leave the boy to be found, always providing those trackers were friendly to Vandy. And he honestly doubted he could get far carrying the boy.

How long had that sound been reaching his ears without his being conscious of it? Nik shifted Vandy's body to free his right hand for the blaster. It came from the down side of their island hill where the rain lake washed—a splashing, not just the normal rippling of wind-ruffled water lapping the shoreline.

Nik inched along the ledge, hoping to see what lay below. And it was not too difficult to make out a bulk floundering there, not swimming, but wading through shallows, staggering now and then, once going to its knees and rising with an exclamation.

A man!

Nik stiffened, watched. By all he could discover, the wader was alone. Coming in that direction, he could well be from the flitter that had fled the refuge in the last moments of battle.

The man reached the shore of the rain lake and steadied himself with one outflung hand against a rock. He looked up as if searching the island hill for hand holds. Cin-goggles made a mask to conceal his face, but this was not Orkhad or any of his race.

Plainly, the stranger decided the rise before him unclimbable. He began to move along it, still supporting himself with one hand against the rock wall. Now that he was free of the water, Nik saw he was limping, pausing now and again as if the effort to keep moving was a heavy one.

He neared the place where Nik and Vandy had climbed. Would that tempt him also? Vandy was quiet. Carefully, Nik laid him down against the crest that crowned the hill. He waited in silence for the stranger's next move.

"Hacon?"

Startled, Nik glanced, at Vandy, but that had not come from the boy. The low hail sounded from below! And only one person other than Vandy would have called him by that name. Eagerly Nik leaned over the edge of the ledge and stared down at that goggle-masked, upturned face.

"Captain Leeds!"

"In person. But not quite undamaged. In fact, I don't believe I can make that perch of yours without a hand up—and we may all need a perch soon!"

"They're after you?"

"Oh, not the Patrol, if that's what you mean. No, this mismade hell world has its own hunters, and a couple of them have been sniffing up my trail for longer than I care to remember."

Nik scrambled down the slope. The captain's hand fell on his arm, and he gave support to the other's weight.

"You're hurt badly?"

"Wrenched my leg when I took a tumble some distance back there. Couldn't favor it much after I fought off that night lizard. Knew the rest of its clutch would be coming. And they were—at least two of them! You have any arms at all?"

"Two blasters. Don't know how much charge they have left."

"Two blasters—that's about the most comforting news I've had since I lifted off Korwar. Talk about luck—we've got a lot of it now—mostly all bad.

"First, that Patrol snoop ray picked me up on the big orbit in; then they were able to slam three ships after me before my rocket tubes had cooled. Feel as if I've been doing nothing but running for days now. Give us a hand up—"

Somehow, they made it up, but Nik sensed that Leeds must be close to the end of his strength. The captain gave a grunt as Nik settled him on their perch, but a moment later he crawled back to the edge and examined the terrain below.

102

"Couldn't have picked it better myself, boy. Any crawler trying to claw us out of here can only come up this way, and we'll burn out his engine before he gets within clawing distance. What's wrong with the boy here?" He looked back at Vandy.

Nik explained about the disastrous meal of Disian fish.

"No off-world supplies, eh?" Leeds asked.

"No. I left the containers I had back at the tunnel break." Hurriedly, Nik outlined the main points of their flight for Leeds.

"That's going to complicate matters," the captain said. "Vandy's conditioned—"

"Conditioned?" Nik repeated uncomprehendingly.

"I told you, he is conditioned all the way—against going with strangers, against everything that would make it easy to lift him out of HS."

"But he ate what was in those rations without trouble."

"Those are LB supplies—emergency food. No one of Terran ancestry can be conditioned against those. It's an elementary precaution rigidly kept. Suppose Vandy's spacer had been wrecked on the way to Korwar—there would be a chance of escape by LB. So he could eat LB rations. Now, he can't eat anything else—on this world."

"But—" Nik realized the futility of his protest. Without LB rations, Vandy would starve. And the LB rations, the cans he had driven into the wall of that cut to serve as a stairway and then abandoned thoughtlessly, were far behind. Those containers meant Vandy's life—unless there were other supplies he could tap.

"Yes"—Leeds pushed back from the rim of the ledge to set his shoulders against the crest rise—"it presents a problem, doesn't it? But there is a solution. Vandy's our way out of here."

"How?" Nik demanded.

"The Patrol—they've taken the refuge. Probably some scout squad is out there now hunting down my flitter. They'll track me here, and then—then we'll have our bargaining point, Vandy for our freedom. Boy, you gave both of us about the best break in this whole bungled job when you lit out with Vandy. Him for us—my spacer, free air out of here— Yes, I thought you were a gift from Lady Luck; now I know that's the truth! We have the boy—so all our comets slid over their stars on the table. You ever play star and comet, Nik."

"No."

"Well, it's a game of chance they tell you—sure, it is. But there's skill to it—real skill—and most of that lies in selecting the right opponents and knowing just how far they're ready to plunge in answer to any bet you're reckless enough to make. I know how far the Patrol will go to get Vandy back—and it's pretty near all the way. He's about the most important pawn in a big-system game going on right now, so much so that the orders from our top were to erase him—"

"Erase him?" Nik echoed.

"Sure, the Guild deal was to take him out of the game permanently. These Gallardi—they're very family and bloodline conscious. The boy's father is the warlord who's holding the key stronghold on Ebo. To wipe out his family line would mean he would then make some suicide play—"

"But Vandy's father is dead—" Nik said bewildered. His hand was at his chin, cupping the firm bone and smooth flesh he needed for reassurance. Leeds' story, which had bought him that face—

"On the contrary, Jerrel Naudhin i'Arkrama was very much alive the last I heard. At least, he was to Lik Iskhag, which was the important point as far as the Guild was concerned. Iskhag paid to have the Naudhin i'Akrama line finished—"

"Then the story you told me—"

Leeds shrugged impatiently. "Was a story, a good one. I didn't know I had it in me to do a regular tape-type tale. Only now it's all worked out for the best, anyway. We can use Vandy to get out of here. And—believe me, Nik—I had my own ideas about the boy and this erase order all the time. Of course, his being conditioned meant trouble, but he could have been kept under wraps until Iskhag got what he paid for—the surrender of the garrison on Ebo. Then Vandy could have been turned loose. I don't hold with erasing children any more than you do. Orkhad's being here wasn't part of the plan as I was told it, either. But maybe it was good that he was—he made you take to the hills, and that certainly saved Vandy. Now, all we have to do is wait for the Patrol to get a direction on us and argue it out—"

"And if they do come," Nik asked, "do you plan to turn the boy over to them on their word to carry out their bargain?"

Leeds laughed. "No—I'm no fool, and neither do I think you're one, Nik. We get the spacer and free air, Vandy going with us. Outside, we put him in a suit with a beeper and space him. They can easily pick him up on a directional signal. And by the time they've retrieved him, we're in the clear and long gone. The plan isn't completely free of a misfire, but it's the best chance we have now."

"And if they don't find us, Vandy has to have food." Nik stated the immediate problem. Leeds had talked a lot, and he wanted to think it over.

The captain moved his shoulders against the rock support.

"Yes, let me think about that. I took a jump from the flitter, and she fire-smashed out there. The emergency rations on board must have gone up with the machine. Those you left back in the cut seem our best chance now. Of course, the Patrol might already have prowled that area and found your trail. But it's still the quickest way—"

"You mean—I go after them?"

"Seeing as how I can probably not even make it down from this ledge again for a while, I'd say you are Vandy's only chance of getting some food in the immediate future. If you are picked up by the Patrol, you still have your chance, and a good one. I'll be here with the boy, and I'll swear by anything you want that any bargain I'll make is for the both of us! That's the truth. I wouldn't be in any position to bargain if I didn't have Vandy. And who gave him to me—you did! We get out together. And if you are netted, you tell the truth—that you know where Vandy is and that he will be delivered safe and sound on our terms. Anyway, we're small fry in this as far as the Patrol is concerned. They want Iskhag, those behind *him,* the man who made the bargain in the first place. You can say I'll give some help in that direction—I don't like the erase plan enough to cover up for those who gave such an order.

"But you may be really lucky and get in and out of there without getting caught, or least only picking up a tracker, and if you do that, it will be just what we want, anyhow."

Leeds leaned over to touch Vandy's forehead.

"Guess he's asleep now, but you can tell them if they pick you up, that he's none too happy. Could just hurry the whole matter along, and that would suit us all."

Nik sat quietly. Again everything Leeds said made good sense, good sense if you accepted his new story and its logic. But to do so meant leaving Vandy here with Leeds—the two of them alone—and going straight back into trouble himself. And how could he be sure that this story was any more the truth than that other this same man had told him back on Korwar? Perhaps Leeds had followed that same thought, for now the captain said:

"Nik, you're rubbing that face of yours. Still smooth and real, isn't it? Mightn't be for long—remember? Of course, maybe Gyna did a lasting job, but she said the odds were against that. You want to go back to the Dipple and no face?"

"But if we get out of here, the Guild won't do anything for someone who has helped to spoil a job." Nik had found the flaw in that argument.

For a moment, he thought he had Leeds, but the silence did not last long enough to suggest that the captain did not have a ready reply.

"This was a job split—don't you think that an erase

106

on a child has blast backs at the top? I had *my* backers, too—and you did just what you promised, brought Vandy here. The minute you landed on Dis, you'd done your part. Most of this mix-up was Orkhad's doing, and he was being watched already from above. You played straight, and that makes it a Guild promise for you. Just let us get off-world, and you'll keep your face. But if we sit this out too long or fail—" He shook his head slowly. "So, you see you have a big stake in this, too. You kept your part of the bargain; the Guild will keep theirs."

In the end, it all added up to just one sum, Nik saw, and that was his job. Vandy could not live without food; the nearest available food was back at the refuge. Leeds was too injured to make the trip, so Nik had to go. He looked out at the back trail.

Even with the goggles, the Disian night was too dark for him to see much, and there were hunters in that dark. He was tired from the long day's travel, and a tired man makes errors of judgment, is duller of sight and hearing. It was not going to be easy, and he wanted every possible advantage on his side.

"I'll go—in the morning."

"Fair enough!" Leeds moved against his back support. "No use going it blind. Maybe we'll be lucky and they'll reach us by then."

Vandy rolled over. "Hacon—" His voice was a husky whisper.

"Here," Nik answered quickly.

"I'm thirsty—"

Leeds pulled a canteen from his belt. "Filled this down there at the lake. Give him a pull."

Nik supported the boy with one arm and held the canteen to his lips while Vandy drank in gulps. Then he pushed the container away.

"I hurt," he said, "right here." His hand moved across his mid-section. "Guess I was pretty sick."

"Yes," Nik agreed. "You try to get some sleep now, Vandy."

But the boy had struggled up a little. "There's someone else here." His head swung around toward Leeds, and his eyes were wide and staring. "There is, isn't there!" That was more demand than question.

"Yes," Nik told him. "Captain Leeds' flitter crashed out there. He just got here."

"Captain Leeds," Vandy repeated. "He's one of them, one of the men back in that tunnel place—"

"Not one of those who were there, Vandy. He's the one we've been waiting for."

Vandy pawed at Nik's arm and strove to raise himself higher.

"He's one of them!" That was accusation rather than recognition.

"No." Nik thought fast. If Vandy looked upon the captain as his enemy, he would not be willing to remain here while Nik backtracked in the morning. "No." He repeated that denial with all the firmness he could summon. "Captain Leeds was trying to find us, to get us out of here. He *is* a friend, Vandy."

"But he's one of them back there—"

"He only pretended to be, Vandy." Nik sought wildly for a plausible explanation. "He was coming here to help us; that's why we were hiding out here. Remember? We were waiting for Captain Leeds. And he was driven out by them, too. He's been hurt and can't walk far—"

"Hacon." Vandy turned in Nik's hold, his eyes now striving to the other's face above him. "You swear that—by the Three Words?"

All that past Vandy had created for his chosen companion tightened around Nik. Vandy's faith was not that of Nik Kolherne nor of the Dipple, but it was a firm bastion for him, and he had made it a part of the world he had imagined for Hacon. Now Nik found his indoctrination in that fantasy had brought a measure of belief to him. He dared not hesitate, but as he answered, he knew the bitterness of his lie.

"I swear it—by the Three Words!" His left hand at his face pressed tight enough against the rebuilt flesh to bring pain. Hacon's face—and to Vandy he was Hacon.

"Believe him now, Vandy?" Leeds asked, his voice holding the same light, cheerful note that Nik had heard in it at their earlier meetings. "It's true. I came here to help the two of you. But I ran into more trouble than I expected, so now I'm tied to this perch of yours for a while. We'll have to hold this garrison together for Hacon—"

"Hacon!" Vandy's fingers were a tight grasp on him. "Where are you going?"

"As soon as day comes, I'm scouting." Nik had no idea whether or not Vandy was aware of his conditioning. At least, the boy had not mentioned it when Nik had urged the fish on him. And if he did not know, there was no good reason to frighten him when off-world supplies were still out of reach.

"But why?" Vandy was protesting, his tight clutch on Nik continuing.

"Because Captain Leeds may have been trailed. We need to know just how much trouble to expect." That was thin but the best Nik could concoct at that moment.

"Yes, just to scout and to pick up some supplies I cached when my leg gave out," Leeds added with his usual facility for invention.

"Oh." A little of that desperate grip lessened, and Vandy's head fell back on Nik's arm. "In the morning—not now?"

"In the morning," Nik agreed, "not now."

11

Nik fought a desire to turn and look back at the island hillock. The humid air was thick about him, though the storm streams had drained away, leaving only the cuts of their passage in the old sea bed. There was no sunrise visible on this cloud-shrouded planet, but the steam mists of the day before were not so thick, most of them confined to the yet lower level where the rain lake lay. He could see ahead and around enough to mark any lizard such as Leeds had fled from or the furred things out of the ruins.

As he went, Nik tried to imagine what Dis had been like before the sun flare had steamed up the seas and rivers and wracked the very bones of the planet with quakes and eruptions. It had always, of course, been a dim world by the standards of his own species. But to its natives, the infrared sun must have been as clear as the yellow-white stars were normal to Nik's kind. And it had been a civilized world, judging by the ruins. The high quality of art shown in the statues of the watchers and their humanoid companion testified to the height of that civilization.

Disians had tried to escape the wrath of their heavens by retreat to the refuge. Had any survivors lingered on in those prepared depths to waver forth again into a ruined outer world? Did any still exist anywhere on Dis? Nik had tried to pry out of Leeds during the early hours of the night some information concerning this planet, knowing that any scrap might mean, by force of circumstances, life or death for him. But the captain had said, "I don't know," to most of his questions.

Dis's first discovery had one of those by-chance things. A Free Trader before the war, threatened by a power leakage, had streaked for the nearest planet recorded on their instruments and set down here. And because it was a Free Trader and not a Survey ship that had made the discovery, there had been no official report, the Traders seeing a profit in their knowledge. Traders formerly dealt with the Guild on occasion when that organization had a quasi-legal standing or when there was no chance of being drawn into trouble by such contact. Thus Dis had become an article of trade.

Leeds' own exploration had brought him knowledge of the refuge and had given the Guild an excellent base hideout—a hideout, Nik gathered, although Leeds was evasive on that point, within cruising distance of several systems in which the Guild had extensive dealings. But once the refuge had been stocked and was in use, the rest of Dis's outer shell was of little or no interest to the outlaws. In fact, they had a kind of horror of it built up by several accidents and encounters with its native fauna, which led them to use it to discipline any rebels. Being set loose on the surface without cin-goggles or weapons was an ultimate punishment.

So—only a small portion of Dis was known to those who used it. Were it not that Vandy was conditioned, they could have taken to the outlands and been safe. Safe from whom, another part of Nik questioned. The Patrol was here to get Vandy, to return him to his people. No, Vandy did not need to hide out in the wilds. That was Nik's portion and Leeds'. Yet the captain was so sure they could strike a bargain for their own benefit.

Nik had been seeing it for several moments before he realized that a bush to his left and ahead was not quite right. Right? Why did he think that? He paused and surveyed the growth closely for a moment or two until he understood what made the difference. It was the color! All the fungoid vegetation he had seen was, to some degree, phosphorescent, with a wan gleam of green or red. This bush had a warmer, yellow tinge.

And—

The color moved!

The yellow had been close to the ground on the left side at first, but it was now halfway up and in the middle, while the first portion had faded to wan glow. Now, the yellow was on the right!

It was not a question of a change in color—Nik was certain of that. But something behind the bush or within its fleshy branches had moved from one position of concealment to another, always keeping well under cover.

Nik tried an experiment. He circled back a little to the left, heading in a direction to take him to the back of the bush. Would the lurker move to face him? Yes! The glow turned with him almost at ground level, keeping pace with him.

Why the presence of that color should be so disturbing, Nik could not have explained. Was it because the source never came into view? Was that thing in ambush aware Nik was able to see it? Perhaps it did now guess because of his own movements.

He looked from the bush in question to others of its kind ahead and saw what he feared and expected. Three of those growths had the betraying glow. To avoid them, he would have to advance to the very edge of the drop to the next level. He could not bring himself to approach any closer to what might be a trap.

There was the blaster. He could here and now burn that nearest bush and its inhabitant into charred powder, but to attack heedlessly was no answer either. He held the weapon ready as he started along the cliff rim.

It was then that Nik heard the whistle, a piping call that was like a throb of pain beginning in his head and running along his nerves to make his flesh tingle. Three times that shattering call came. Now the lights in the bushes were steady; all faced him. Nik knew the menace of a before-attack. Were these the furred hunters? He did not believe so. But what?

To keep on along the edge of the drop now was to expose himself to a rush. But how else dared he advance?

It was coming—now! How Nik knew that, he could not have told. But he leaped into an open space where any attackers would be exposed to blaster fire.

The bushes shook, spilling the lurkers into sight. They came scuttling, at first on hands and knees. Then, from a crouch, they launched themselves at him—or two of them did, while three remained in reserve. Nik had expected animals, but these—these were men!

"No!" He heard his own involuntary cry, but the others ran mute.

And he saw that he was not confronting new refugees from the Guild base or Patrol scouts. These were naked, thin ghostly creatures. The foremost carried a club in the head of which had been set a row of ugly projections. His companion held a stone as big as his own head.

They sped toward the off-worlder, their eyes agleam with a terrible insanity. Nik fired, almost without consciously willing that push of the finger. The club carrier went down, and at the same time that throb of a whistle beat in Nik's brain and made his hands quiver and shake.

The second attacker stopped short when his companion fell. He retreated a step or two to stand over his body. His head swung from side to side, his nostrils expanding visibly as if to soak up some necessary scent.

On his bare body the glowing skin was stretched over a rack of bones. And there was no trace of hair on face, head, or body. The features on the face now swinging back toward Nik were roughly human, though the nose was very wide and flat, the nostrils large pits. The mouth was also wide; the lips were thin, rolled back in a snarl to display large, sharp teeth, while the eyes were sunk back into the skull, difficult to see in their twin caverns.

The stranger dropped his stone weapon, tossing it carelessly aside, where it was speedily pounced upon by one of the smaller lurkers. He wrested the club from the flaccid fingers of the dead one and swung it once or twice, as if testing its balance.

Nik tensed, waiting for a second rush, but the other made no move to renew hostilities. He backed away toward the bushes, keeping a wary eye on Nik, his three companions going to ground more quickly. Then as suddenly as they had appeared, they were gone, leaving the dead behind.

Who—or what? Nik knew of the prisoners who had been driven out of the refuge. But surely, humanoid though these creatures appeared, they were not of off-world stock! He marked their going in the bush glow, but they did not retreat far. Those betraying patches of light squatted, each in a hiding place, along the path he must take. Whatever the purpose of that attack, it had not been abandoned as far as the Disians were concerned. But they would not try a second rush into blaster fire.

Should he detour down to the second level of the sea bottom and climb again when he reached the old seaport? There was no reason to fear the outcome, even if all four rushed him; yet Nik shrank from a second battle. Whatever or whoever the strangers were, they were human enough to seem remotely of his kind. And to meet a club and a stone with a blaster was sheer butchery in Nik's mind. At the same time, he did not doubt that the Disians had no parallel qualms. Did they know that a body light revealed them to him, or were they unaware of that disadvantage?

Nik studied the ground ahead. The growth of vegetation that favored the concealment of the strangers did not extend too far. If he could keep on along the cliff edge and so come in to the open, he might avoid another encounter.

He broke into a trot, covering that area of inherent

peril with what speed he could. Such exertion in this humidity left him gasping, staggering a little, as he burst into the welcome open. With one hand pressed against his laboring chest, he looked behind. The lights—they were moving again, not directly after him but for the cliff face of the old shoreline. He stood watching those now distant figures break from the brush cover and begin to climb the wall with the agility of those who had performed that particular maneuver before. Had they abandoned the chase?

No goggles on their faces—they *must* be native to this world! Were they degenerate remnants of the race that had fashioned the refuge, survivors of the catastrophe that had wrecked Dis? Goggles—Nik's hand went up to touch the ones he wore. Those were a very fragile hold on life. Just suppose he were to break or lose the cins—he would be easy prey for even a club man then. He drew a ragged breath and tried to quiet the pounding of his labored heart.

There ahead was where the winged fighters had battled over their prey, and that far the furred hunters had come. Nik examined the ground carefully. There was no cover he could detect large enough to screen one of the furred beasts, but he kept the blaster in his hand. As he turned to set out, he caught a last glimpse of the Disians. The club man was near the top of the cliff, and he, in turn, was looking down at Nik, watching the off-worlder with intent interest. Then his glowing body was up and over that last rise, and he was gone. But Nik had a strong feeling he was not abandoning the chase.

A pile of well-cleaned bones marked the place where the furred hunters had feasted, but there was no other sign of them. Nik forged ahead. He was in comparatively clear territory here, and his next landmark was the reef, though that was yet a good journey beyond. From there the climb into the city ruins— The city ruins! If there ever was a perfect place to lay an ambush, it was there—right there.

Nik tried to remember what he had seen of the ruins,

to think whether there was some other way around them to reach the tunnel break of the refuge. But he was afraid that if he avoided the obvious landmarks, he might become hopelessly lost. There was something frightening about launching out into the open sea bottom away from the old shoreline. With those cliffs at hand, the reef ahead, he had a sense of security, of knowing in part what he could expect. He decided that he would retrace the path he and Vandy had taken earlier.

The coarse, gravelly soil slipped and slid under his boots as it had not earlier. He guessed that the moisture had drained out of it, leaving it the texture of sand, making walking just that much harder. His lungs still labored to separate air from the dankness, and he cut his pace.

There was no more commotion in the rain lake below. There were no winged fishers, no signs of turmoil in the waters, which had receded a goodly distance from where they had been at the end of the storm. In the midst of one such dry part, a glint caught Nik's attention, and he wavered to a stop. This was tangled wreckage, not a rock outcrop. It was something fashioned long ago by intelligence—a ship, surface or air transportation of some kind. Metal had gone into its making and gave back now that sullen glint of light.

It was still in sight when Nik knocked over a small creature with a thrown stone. He found himself holding a limp body with rudimentary leather wing flaps stretching between its front and rear legs, and that body was scaled. Trying not to think of its alien form, he skinned and cleaned it. Then he choked down mouthfuls of the rank-tasting flesh. Food was fuel, and fuel his body needed; he could not be dainty in his eating.

On again—the reef was ahead, and in the reef he would shelter by nightfall, preferring it to the ruins. He could not do without sleep forever. It was getting harder to think clearly. Nik halted, his hand going to his head. That throb! It was like something—the whistle call of the Disians!

Slowly, staggering a little, he turned about to view the cliff top to his left. Rock—that was all, just rock. No club wielder was climbing down again. But the muddle in his head—that throb which was more pain than sound—

The reef—he would get to the reef and hole up there. It was darkening; it must be close to the day's end. He could see the reef, a black streak across the dull sea bottom. Nik wavered on, the gritty soil slipping under his feet so that once he fell to one knee and found it difficult to scramble up again.

He feared a return of that throb in his head, shrinking from the very thought of it. His hand shook so that he had to belt hook the blaster. Was he sick from that food he had forced into him as Vandy had been sick the night before? There was something wrong—very wrong—

Once Nik swung around to go back, back to the island hill and Leeds and Vandy. But then he knew that he could not make it. It would be better to reach the reef and rest there. The crevice in which he and Vandy had sheltered beckoned him. Just get there and rest—rest— His hand wiped back and forth across his face. Once that movement pushed aside the goggles, and he cried out in fear as his sight was distorted. He was no longer truly conscious of what was happening to him, only that apprehension was clouding his mind and that the thought of the hiding hole in the reef kept him moving.

The rest of that day was a haze for Nik. But he roused when he lurched up against a rock and looked a little stupidly at a wall of them. He had reached the reef, he thought foggily. The reef—safety—rest— If he could only crawl a little farther!

There were bright glints of light—or eyes, eyes watching—waiting—assessing his fatigue, his bemused mind? Was it that additional prick of fear that pulled Nik farther out of the fog? Something gave him power enough to drag himself up, along the rocks, heading for the pocket he remembered.

He kicked away something that rattled against the stone and saw a claw-tipped bone flip up and away from his stumbling feet—the remains of the crawler he had blasted before their crevice camp. So, he was almost there now.

The glint of eyes—they were still at a distance. His sobbing breaths beat in his own ears, so that he could not hear anything that might be creeping up for the kill.

Just a little farther. Now—hold on to this rock, pull up to the next, an irregular stairway to the crevice. He reeled back against the very boulder where he had kept sentry two days earlier.

Once more he drew blaster fumblingly and laid it on the rock. His hands still shook, but he could use both of them to bring that weapon into play against the eyes—

A small part of Nik's mind was aroused enough now to wonder at his present half collapse. There was no real reason for him to be so exhausted, so dazed. Ever since that whistling when he had encountered the Disians— Nik rubbed his hand across his forehead, pressing the goggles painfully against his skin. No, he must not disturb those! He jerked his fingers away.

He was so tired that he could not keep his feet—yet those waiting eyes— Sobbing a little, Nik wedged himself erect, dimly thinking that any attack would be limited to a narrow front he could defend. But how long could he continue to keep watch?

His head fell forward; he was floating—floating on a shifting mist that enfolded, engulfed him, spun him out and out—

Pain throbbed from his head down into his back and arms. Nik's head snapped up and back and struck against stone with shock enough to bring him out of that mist. The throb—but he was alert enough to see the thing working its way among the rocks, a shadow advancing from deeper shadows. He clutched the blaster and tried to press the firing button.

The ray shot across the top of the barrier dock. It missed the creeper but sent it into retreat. Nik dragged himself forward. He had to meet what was coming in the open. He had to!

His forward effort succeeded. Eyes—yes, there were the eyes again—one pair, two, more— He could not count them now—they spun, danced, jerked about in a crazy pattern when he tried to watch.

Nik cried out as another throb burst in his head. All those eyes—they were uniting into one! No! He was wrong—not eyes but a light! An honest light—not of Dis— He had only to follow that to safety.

He pushed away from the rock and crept around, angry that his body obeyed his will so sluggishly. He must hurry, must run to the light that meant an end to nightmares—only let him reach the light!

12

The light was receding!

"Wait!" Nik got that out in a cry close to a scream.

And it appeared that the light did steady. He was far past wondering about its source. He believed only that it spelled safety. But his feet would not obey his will. He fell heavily, then tried to force his body up again, his attention all for the light.

Shouting— Through the fog in his head, he thought he could hear words, understandable words—yet they were too far away, too confused to count as did the light. Nik began to crawl.

He was close, too close, when the enchantment of the light failed, when he fronted the horror behind that mask. A Disian! Nik had a momentary glimpse of a naked body rising from behind another form, a dense, hairy blot from which wavered and sparkled the light. A memory, so vague that Nik could not hold it, came and went in a second—a fisher that used light for bait? When and where?

Then he was overborne by the attack, smelled the reek of alien body scent, and was pinned flat to the ground under the full weight of the other's spring. Nik struggled feebly against that hold, but there was no escape. And always the throb in his head and body grew stronger until he shook and quivered with its beat.

The weight on his back and shoulders was suddenly still, so still that one of Nik's squirms detached its hold. He made a greater effort and tried to pull free.

The Disian collapsed in a limp tangle of limbs, still half pinning Nik, but from under which he was able to crawl. He sat up and strove to find the blaster, but his groping hand encountered only empty hooks. Had he had it when he left the rocks? He could not remember.

He jerked his feet from under the flaccid sprawl of the Disian. Why the other had gone down was beyond Nik's reasoning now. But that he had another chance, small as it might be, penetrated enough to send him scrabbling, still on hands and knees, back from that spot.

Things flowed up from the reef rocks, seeming to grow out of the ground about—creatures that could not have life, that were out of off-world nightmares or of Vandy's fantasies with which they had clogged his brain! Nik was the focus of a weird, menacing ring, and the ring was drawing in.

Nik gave a shriek of pure terror, pushed for a second almost over the border of sanity. He screamed again, but he also threw himself at the nearest of those monsters, driven to meet it rather than to wait for its spring. Raking claws in his face—pain—

How far can one retreat from horror into oneself? Was it exhausted sleep that held Nik or a kind of withdrawal from what he could not face? He came out of that suspension little by little, with a reluctance of which he was quite aware.

And because of that reluctance, he did not dare to move, to try to use his mind or his senses, lest he find himself back again in that circle of monstrous life.

How soon did that first small hint of reason awake? When did he note that the air he was drawing into his lungs was not water-soaked so that he must labor to get a full breath? How long had it been since he had breathed so effortlessly—and felt this cool and dry?

Or was this all part of some dream that would make the waking that much the worse for him? But perhaps it was the air that was clearing his mind as well as his lungs.

Fresh air—the refuge! He was back in the refuge,

and with that guess he unlocked memory. But, the refuge was in the hands of the enemy—which meant he was now a prisoner.

For the first time, Nik willed his hand to move, only to panic when no muscle obeyed. This was not like the sapped exhaustion of his last confused recollection—this was a new helplessness. And once before he had been so frozen—when Leeds had taken him captive in the Dipple! He was a prisoner all right!

Now, as at that previous time, Nik tried to make his ears serve to give him some idea of his surroundings. The swish-swish of the air was easy to identify. But there were other sounds, too, some close, some distant. He heard a clicking in regular pattern, and he thought it marked the action of some machine or installation. Then there was another sound, followed by the snap of space boot plate soles hitting the floor. Someone was walking, not toward him, however. That snapping drew farther away. Was he alone now or were there others in the room? The swish of air covered any sound of breathing.

So, he was a prisoner in stass—which meant his body was pinned here helplessly—but his mind was no longer blanked out. How much of the immediate past was illusion and how much truth? He had certainly reached the reef and then been drawn out of that poor safety by the light. And the Disians had done that.

Then—what had happened? The blackout of his Disian attacker—did Nik owe that to his present captors? Had they witnessed that battle and saved him for their own purposes? There was logic in that.

So the Patrol had him. But they wanted Vandy, and there was a time limit on Vandy, giving Nik a talking point—unless they had already backtracked on him and made their own deal with Leeds—

Nik's mouth was very dry; he tried to flex his lips, to move his tongue, without success. This stass was complete.

There—more footfalls, and now the murmur of voices, voices speaking Basic, one with an accent.

This time the steps came up to where he lay—two people, Nik was sure.

There was silence for a long moment. They must be studying him—trying to learn if he had aroused to consciousness yet.

"Amazing—" That was the accented voice. "The one thing we did not foresee."

There was a sharp answering sound, which might have been an exclamation of anger or even a laugh without much humor.

"We long ago discovered, Commander, that there is so often something unforeseen. Perfection is an ending very far in the future, if we ever reach that state. No, this was hardly to be foreseen, but it worked—very well, if we are to judge by the results we have had to face so far. You've seen the tape we discovered. And that was probably only one of many; it would have to be under the circumstances. You can't cut off a small boy from all companionship on his own age level. If you don't provide a friend, he will have one, even in his own mind. So, we have Hacon here—"

"Yes, we have *him!*"

Nik's bonds would not allow any physical reaction to the menace in that voice, the promise of ill to come in the emphasis on *him*.

"Remember, Commander, he's our route to your young charge. He took the boy out of here before our attack, some time before it. You recall the testimony?"

"But you found him out there alone!"

"We found him coming back."

"Which means?"

"Probably that he was returning to set up a deal. There may have been more than one of these rats who took to the open before the end. If any of them were on Veep level or even had brains enough to do some moderate thinking, they'd want a deal. And they have only one thing to bargain with—the boy. So to send this bait of theirs back would be the logical move in opening negotiations."

"To bargain with such filth!"

"Commander, this is a big planet and an unknown one as far as we are concerned. You say the boy was fully conditioned, which means he'll need off-world food. They can't have too much of it out there. And they can be hiding anywhere. We have one radiation tracker, and that won't work—you saw it fail. This Dis is too far off our norm. Adjustments to the machine can be made, but that all takes time. With a conditioned boy held by desperate men, how much time do we have?"

"Then you say to bargain?"

"I say that the first consideration is the boy's safety. If that can be obtained by a bargain—we had better bargain."

"And afterwards?"

"Afterwards—we shall keep to the strict letter of any bargain, Commander, but the strict letter will not deter future action against those responsible for this. After all, this prisoner here was only a tool. Do you want just the hands? Is it not better to wait and take the brain behind them?"

"To bargain—" The disgust was plain. "But you are right, of course. How soon do we get to it—this bargaining?"

"At once!"

The stiff shell that had encased Nik was gone. They had loosed the stass. He opened his eyes and lay staring up at the two men.

One wore the black tunic of the Patrol, the diamond double star of a squadron leader on his collar. The other was brown of skin, and his hair was as dark as Vandy's. He was plainly of the same race as the boy. He too wore a uniform, more colorful than the Patrol officer's, and there was the glitter of decoration links on the breast of his dark red tunic. He stared back at Nik with a hatred and contempt that was hot and bitter, expressed in his eyes and the twist of his lips. The Patrolman had a calm detachment about the prisoner that was in a way just as forbidding. Nik was very glad he had had those moments to think ahead. The man in red spoke first.

124

"Where is the boy?"

Nik wet his dry lips with his tongue. His mouth felt cottony, so dry that he was not sure he could answer audibly. But matters were moving just as Leeds had foreseen. Vandy was their bargaining point, and both these men were ready to accept that. He swallowed and found a whisper of voice.

"Safe—so far—"

"I asked—where?"

Nik was too close yet to stass stiffness to avoid that blow. It cracked against his face, almost battering him back into dizzy half consciousness. When he was able to focus again, he saw that the Patrolman had a grip on that red clothed arm and had pinned it to the other's side.

"That won't do—any—good—" Nik was battling for more than Leeds' bargain now. He had no doubt that this commander, whoever he was, would try to beat the information out of him. He had to appeal to logic on the part of the Patrolman. "I'm not the one giving the orders—out there—"

"But you do know where he is? You were sent here to bargain—" said the Patrolman.

"No, came for food." Nik rubbed a trickle of blood from the corner of his mouth. "Vandy has to have food—"

"You—!" The commander lunged at him, and the Patrol officer twisted between them.

"i'Inad! Calm down, man. So you have no off-world supplies?"

"Not enough—and the boy can't eat native food."

"Then, by the Three Names," the commander exploded, "bring him back!"

He would like nothing better, Nik wanted to say. But there was the bargain—Vandy for a ship, a clear start—safety for Leeds and for Nik Kolherne.

"Why did you run with the boy in the first place?"

That question was so unexpected that Nik answered the Patrolman with the truth.

"They wanted to kill him—"

"Who did?"

There was no point in not telling the rest of it.

"A Veep called Orkhad. He was in command here."

"What did you expect to accomplish by running? There was no place to run to—or was there?" The Patrolman made that a question. "Another nest waiting?"

"Not that I know of," Nik returned promptly. To tell all the truth that did not apply to Leeds and their present precarious position was, he believed, his best move. For all he knew, they could have him, probably did have him, under a scanner now. If he supplied the truth in most things, they would be more likely to listen to him.

"So you just went out on the surface with the boy to hide out. What did you hope to gain?"

"I was expecting someone to come, someone who could overrule Orkhad." Again the full truth.

"A division in their ranks, eh?" The Patrolman did not question that.

"I don't know." Nik chose his words with care. "But Orkhad was not following the orders I had been given."

"Which were?"

The truth—if they did have a scanner on him, they would know he spoke the truth. And he was sure they had him under such observation.

"To keep Vandy safe—for the information he had—"

Commander i'Inad moved closer. "Vandy—information?" he repeated. "But the boy has no information they couldn't have learned by other sources. That's a lie!"

The Patrolman had turned his head, and Nik followed that line of sight. The machine that had been clicking away so steadily—he had never seen a scanner, but he was sure that was one. And now the Patrolman proved Nik correct.

"No, that is the truth as far as this one knows. What kind of information?"

Again Nik told them the truth. He put Leeds' first story to him into a few terse sentences. It sounded thin, retold like this, but the scanner would bear him out.

He was developing an affection for that machine—so far.

"And you believed that?" The commander was highly incredulous.

Nik pulled himself up on the bunk where he had been lying.

"I believed it," he returned flatly. There was no use adding that he had wanted to believe it, that he was eager to, considering what acceptance of the story meant to him.

"But when you got here, Orkhad had a different tale?"

"Yes." Nik told them that also.

"So you took the boy and ran for it? Why?"

"It was the only thing to do. I thought we could hide out until the captain came—"

"This captain—Strode Leeds?"

Nik was not surprised when the Patrolman named Leeds. He must have picked up a lot from prisoners taken here in the refuge.

"Yes—Captain Leeds."

"Leeds has the boy now?"

"Yes."

"Where?"

This was the hard part. Could he defeat the scanner by thought? Nik was not sure it could be done, but it was his only chance.

"I can't tell you where; there's no map. But I can take you there." Two full truths—one hedging. Would the whole come out on the truth side in the report?

The commander, as well as the Patrolman, was watching the machine for some confirmation or denial Nik could not read.

"Well?" i'Inad demanded, not of Nik but of the Patrolman.

"True—"

For the first time, Nik's tension eased somewhat. He had beat the scanner by that much. Heartened by that victory, he ventured to prod a little on his own.

"I need food for Vandy—soon—"

"Let's go now!" That was i'Inad.

"Leeds will have the boy where you left him?" The Patrolman was not so quick to pick that suggestion up.

Of that Nik had no doubts. His injury was enough to pin the captain to the island hill. He could not get away and take Vandy with him in the boy's present weak condition, and he would not abandon the one chance he had of buying his freedom. Nik nodded.

"Let's go!" i'Inad repeated. He grabbed at Nik, dragging him off the bunk with a rough jerk.

The Patrolman had crossed the room. Now he returned carrying a container of liquid, which he held out to Nik.

"Drink it!"

Nik surveyed the contents of the cup warily. There were a lot of rumors about the Patrol methods. He had no desire to go out of here drugged, obedient to orders in spite of his will. The green liquid had no odor, but he hesitated even as he held the cup to his lips.

The Patrol officer frowned. "It's no drug—not the kind you fear." He must have read Nik's thoughts or else the scanner reported that, too. "That's Patrol iron rations. You'll need it to keep going."

Nik had to believe him. His own weakness of body when he tried to move warned him that he could not make any such trip on his own. He drank, and the stuff was warm in his mouth, even more heated in his throat, and hot in his stomach as he swallowed.

"We have to have cin-goggles out there," he said. That was his worst remaining fear, that they might refuse to provide him with those. Suppose they would allow him use of goggles from time to time in order to point out landmarks, would keep him blind most of the journey as a prisoner without bonds?

"All right. We have those."

They went through the passage of the refuge, collecting an escort of Patrolmen on the way—six of them. But when they trod a path through rubble to the outside, Nik, in spite of the cins, was totally at a loss.

"Well, which way?" i'Inad wanted to know. "Are you trying to say you can't tell?"

"I can't—from here." Nik told of their escape through the tunnel cut. When he had finished, the Patrol officer nodded.

"All right, we'll go back through that."

"He's stalling!" rapped out the commander.

"No, he couldn't just have walked out with the boy. Such a bolt hole is far more probable. We'll try that tunnel."

Back into the refuge they went, to the terminal of the ancient ways. But in the tunnel no break showed. Instead, they were faced with an effective stopper of earth and rocks.

"Those explosions when you broke in—" Nik found the answer. "They must have plugged this—"

"Clear it," the Patrol officer ordered.

Something more powerful than a blaster ray snapped on, and the barrier melted at its touch. But only more rock and soil poured in.

"That's not going to do it," the officer said a moment later.

"Take a bearing, Dagama. We'll try it over the surface with that as a guide."

Then they were back at the original refuge door, climbing up to the earth, guided by the small cube their advance scout held, which gave off a small beeping sound.

13

They came into the city ruins by the emptied sea basin from a different angle. But once he sighted the shoreline, Nik was confident of his path. As they went through what must once have been streets, he eyed every shadowed rubble cave, every opening leading to darkness. What had truly happened to him back there by the reef, he did not know. That the city had its inhabitants still, he now believed, inhabitants of one kind or another—degenerate Disians or animals.

There was no blaster in his belt hooks, but the rest of the party were armed. And Nik noted that they were as much interested in possible ambush spots as he was. Finally he dared to ask a question.

"How did you find me?"

"Fighting off a hunting party," replied the officer crisply. "One of our scouts had sighted you from the cliff top. He followed along until all at once you came out from some rocks and walked straight at trouble. When they jumped you, Riswold beamed the one who had you down—"

"Then they did fish me out with that light!" Nik was remembering now. "Just as that thing did on the ramp way—"

The officer paid no attention to that, for he was continuing. "Our men picked you up by a reef in that direction."

"Yes, we go down to the sea bottom here and then head that way."

Nik rubbed his head. He had no idea whether this

was morning or evening or of what day. The outward world, even when viewed through goggles, was darkening. And outside the refuge, the humidity again caught them in its soggy grip. Commander i'Inad was breathing in short gasps, and even one or two of the Patrol guard seemed similarly affected. The restorative drink had strengthened Nik, but still he felt as if he were walking thigh deep in water, pushing sluggishly against a strong current that might at any moment sweep him off his footing to be perilously carried away.

They descended to the first level of the sea bottom. Visibility was fading. And then Nik saw the telltale flash on the horizon. Storm! Such a deluge as he had seen before? He stopped to watch the play of lightning.

"What's the matter?"

"Get along with you!" i'Inad caught Nik's shoulder and shoved him on with a force that almost sent him sprawling before he could reply to the Patrol officer's question.

"Storm coming—" Nik got out. "And they're bad here. To be caught in the open—"

The water that had cascaded over the shore cliff, cutting hundreds of swift-flowing streams, to flood this portion of the sea bottom and to build up rain lakes below, how high did that water reach? And if one were caught in the open, could it be fatal? Nik did not know, and he was not eager to find out.

"We'll have to find cover," he told the Patrol officer, knowing he could not appeal to the hostile commander.

"What do you think, Barketh?" i'Inad asked the other. Maybe that play of lightning and the horrible pre-storm smother of humid air made some impression on the commander.

"Planet's weather is definitely unbalanced. Yes, a storm could be nasty. And there're signs this is a drain basin."

"We can't go back!" i'Inad protested. "The boy—we have to reach him soon—if we can believe this—this graxal here!"

"How far is the reef? Can we make that before the storm breaks?"

Nik had no idea, but he did know that this was a time for action and not just stopping to consider what action. He started on at a trot, the best pace he could keep under the weight of the humid air. Yes, the spine of the reef promised shelter of a sort. And, though he had very little experience with Dis's worst, Nik did believe that they needed some protection against the coming fury. How long *did* they have? None of them knew. But no one of that squad attempted to stop him; they only stepped up their own pace to join his flight.

The visibility was shrinking fast. Clouds always hung heavy over Dis, but now the blanket was night-thick, and splinters of lightning dazzled rather than helped their sight. A snarling screech—shadows fleeing across their path gave warning tongue. For several paces, Nik ran beside one of the black furred hunters, and then the Disian animal drew ahead.

Nik's apprehension was as much a weight on his laboring body as the exercise. Had they—or rather he—made the wrong choice? Should they have returned to the ruined city to wait out the storm? He was not even sure now if they were heading in the right direction for the reef.

Flashes that were not of the Disian world stretched paths before them. Nik had forgotten the torches the Patrol must carry. That white-yellow light picked out the creatures that bounded and scuttled-raced for shelter. Another time Nik might have been amazed at the amount of life that had broken out of hiding on the sea bottom. Now he was intent only upon what might lie ahead, on how soon one of those beams would pick up the reef.

The boom of thunder that had begun as a sullen muttering was now creeping closer with a beat that carried a vibration to fill the whole world and even their bodies. It was as confusing in its steady "pound-pound" as that whistling that had bewildered Nik when the Disians had hunted him.

As yet there was no rain, but he feared the buffeting of the torrents when they came. The frenzied flight of the animals about them underlined the danger he suspected.

Rocks stood out more frequently in the path of those flash beams. They must be drawing close to the reef. Then the lightning struck ahead, and the first of the rain came like a blotting curtain to swallow them. Nik saw the flashes of the torches, but he was no longer aware of any of the men near him. A small squealing thing shot between his feet, tripping him up. He fell heavily, to lie gasping the thick air into his laboring lungs, too winded for the moment to regain his feet. A Patrolman loomed out of the murk, stopped and caught at him, tugged him up, and pulled him along for a space.

Water poured down upon them. This was like drowning while one walked on land. Nik flung his arm across his nose and mouth, trying to make a sheltered pocket in which to breathe. He staggered under the weight of water. At least the wind was not as great here as it had been back in the city ruins. He brought up against a rock and clung to it with the same frenzy as a man would embrace an anchor when being borne along in a wild current.

Another Patrolman, or perhaps it was the same one who had aided Nik, blundered up, and this time Nik put out a hand to draw him to that anchorage. Water streamed over them, about them; it gurgled calf high about their legs. There was nothing in the world but the fury of the rain and thunder, the crash and clash of lightning. It was weather gone wild with a force Nik could not have imagined possible.

There was nothing to do but to cling to the rock. To venture on in this was to invite disaster. The Patrolman held to the other side of that anchor with the same grim determination. Water rose about them. Had they come to a stop in the middle of a rain river? It was flowing quickly, pulling at them knee high now. Nik flattened his body against the rough surface of the boulder and put his head on his arm, hoping to breathe better. How much of this could one take? His hands were growing numb. What if he could not keep that hold? Would he be swept by the stream now rising to his thighs? Only a short way on, that stream must plunge over the second cliff to the lower level, doubtless going to feed one of the rain lakes. Hold on—he had to!

Lightning—a flash that was blinding that deadened the senses. Now the wind was coming, driving the rain lashes across the rock and the men, limpet-fast to its sides, a wind that strove to pry them free from those desperate holds, to snap them away in its grasp.

Air—he had to have air to breathe! Nik choked in panic; he fought for each gasp. This was drowning. The water tugged and washed at him now waist high. But to abandon his hold was death, and Nik knew that.

He held, his muscles aching and then going numb, his consciousness retreating into nightmare, and then, past nightmare, into a near blackout. Yet he held on.

A hissing—not steady but broken as if by gasps. Inch by inch, Nik crept back from the refuge into which his mind had retreated. There was still rain, but the wild tumult of the storm was less. He recognized the signs. That hissing—

There was the sharp pain of cramped neck and shoulder muscles as he lifted his head and looked up into a monster's glowing eyes. The thing, squatting on the top of the rock to which Nik clung, flexed its wings and darted its head toward the off-worlder. Nik fell back, his arms and legs too numb to respond naturally.

He splashed into the water. His body was pulled away, though he fought wildly for a handhold, some anchorage. There was a cry—sounding more human than any screech from the winged thing—and a moment later another body came whirling through the water, striking against Nik. Together they were borne helplessly onward until another rock loomed out of the dark and they struck against it, Nik on top.

What followed next was never clear. He was out of

that flood, and so was the other—the Patrolman who had shared his refuge. But the latter lay very still, his body responding a little to the tug of the water. Nik crawled on his hands and knees to what might relatively be termed land. Now without knowing just why, he turned to tug weakly at the other, winning him out of the flood by small pulls.

The rain shrank to a drizzle, but it shadowed the world about them so that Nik could only be sure of what lay within reach. He looked down at the Patrolman who lay face up, the rain glistening on his skin, on his face—!

This was Barketh, and his goggles were gone! Nik's hand flew to his own eyes, just to make sure, though he should have known he would not be able to see this much had his own cins not been in place.

He could see; the Patrolman could not. It was as simple as that. The mishap the other had suffered gave Nik the advantage, and how could he best use it?

Swiftly he transferred the blaster from Barketh's belt to his own empty hooks, then the ration bag— He rolled the body over to free the pouch that had swung from a shoulder strap, terrified lest that also had been lost. No, it had been too securely latched. Each of the Patrol carried supplies, now Nik had this bag, enough to support Vandy for days.

Barketh had been so helpless in his grasp that Nik made a quick examination. The Patrolman was not dead, but a gash on his forehead supplied the reason for his present state. Now Nik had a choice. He could stay where he was and use a blaster to signal his position as soon as the rain subsided, or he could go on with the supplies in freedom.

"Wake up!" He shook Barketh. No need to pour water on the Patrolman; the rain was doing that. But Nik could not drag the other any farther, and neither could he go off and leave a blind and helpless man on the edge of a rain river.

Barketh moaned just as Nik was giving up hope of

bringing him around. He opened his eyes, and his expression changed from vacancy to fear.

"Dark—" Nik had to lean close to hear that word. He spoke distinctly in return.

"Your goggles are gone."

"You—who are you?" Barketh struggled to lever himself up, digging his elbows into the muddy ground.

"I'm Hacon." Nik clung to the name Vandy had given him. "Now listen, the rain is slacking. I've your supply bag, and I'm going on with it. Here's your torch. When you can't feel the rain, shine it as a signal."

But, Nik wondered, would such a signal bring more than just Barketh's men? The furred hunters—the Disians? He felt for the blaster he had taken from the other. To leave a man without a weapon, without cins, alone here—

"You have goggles?" Barketh demanded.

"Yes. But I'm keeping them!"

Barketh felt for his blaster. "You took that, too?"

"Yes. I'm leaving you the torch. And wait—" Nik twisted out of the Patrolman's hold. They could not be too far from the reef. And there Barketh would have shelter. Hurriedly, he explained.

"You won't get far—" the other commented levelly.

"Maybe not, but I have the food, and Vandy needs it. How long would it take you now to get your squad rounded up again, for you to get going?"

"A point—small—but a point. All right, for the time being you give the orders. Stow me away and get going. I agree the boy has to have food."

He held out his hand, but Nik avoided that too easy contact. Reaching behind Barketh, he took hold of the Patrolman's belt and pulled him to his feet. Remaining at the other's back, Nik gave him a small push forward.

"Use your torch," he ordered, "and march."

He had slung the strap of the supply pouch over his own shoulder, where it swung loosely. The light cut a path through the dark, picking up more rock outcrops. Suddenly Nik heard a shout in the murk. He thought it

136

came from above and to the right, as if they had been sighted by some scout who had made the reef. With that he loosed his hold on Barketh's belt, at the same time giving the Patrolman a swift shove, which he hoped would at least momentarily send him off balance and keep him from turning his light on Nik as a target.

As for his own path, he turned left and dodged in and out among rocks, keeping to the best cover he could and heading for the point he must pass. The supply pouch bumped his hip as he ran, and he had the blaster weighing down the carry hooks. By chance alone, he was coming out of this better than he had dared hope.

It was heavy going over the rain-sodden sea bottom. Pools from the drain streams linked here and there into lakes before they drained a second time to the lower level and the waiting "sea" there. Nik had to watch his footing to avoid both water and slick mud and stone. Once or twice a wind gust blew the drizzle so strongly against him that he experienced again the sensation of drowning in water-filled air.

Whether he could be marked by anyone now on the reef, Nik did not know. He went on with a curious tingling between his shoulder blades as if he expected to feel the ray of a blaster beam there. It seemed almost impossible that he would be able to get away without challenge. But he was certain it would not be without pursuit. Nik kept on doggedly, never once looking back, with the odd feeling that his refusal to look for danger in that direction gave him some form of protection.

The heat was rising as the rain slackened, following the pattern of the earlier storm when he and Vandy had seen the mists of steam curling from the ground. Now he smelled an unpleasant odor and moments later came out upon the edge of a great gouge extending from the shore straight across his track. Lightning had struck here and brought about a collapse of the first level of sea bottom. Between Nik and the road he must take to find the island hill was a slash of still-sliding earth and rock.

He went along its verge back to the cliff face, but there was no way to span it here. The rock was too sheer and slippery. Down the center of the gouge splashed a stream, which constantly ate at the stuff of its walls, bringing down more earth slips. He would have to follow it back to the second seaward shelf if he were to cross at all.

That was a nightmare journey, the worst Nik had attempted since he had climbed from the tunnel cut with the unconscious Vandy. Now he had only himself to worry about, but the loosened ground was as treacherous as a whirlpool, and every step started fresh movement.

Nik threw caution aside at last, determined that the only way was to choose his path and then go it with all the speed he could muster to keep ahead of a slide. The debris of the cut carried well out into the second level, and in the basin there the water collected, backing up to keep this disturbed earth fluid and shifting.

He took a deep breath and jumped from ground already moving under his boots to land on a relatively clear space, plunging into slimy soil halfway to his elbows, for he landed on hands and knees. Then he struggled up, rolled down to the verge of the lake, and splashed on with all the energy he could summon for a quick and powerful effort. There was no use trying to breast the other side of the cut. He had been unusually lucky in getting down, but to climb a constantly shifting surface was out of the question.

Nik dodged as a good section of wall gave way, thickening the stream water and sending up spray to fog his goggles. He clawed his way along in what he believed were the shallows, having to depend upon chance and unsure footing. Once he fell as a stone turned under his weight, but luckily the force of the stream was already slackening, and he was able to flounder out before he was carried into the depths of the lake.

Silvery streaks under the surface of the water converged on something floating not too far away. The surface roiled as those streaks fought and lashed. Where the fish had gathered from, Nik did not know, but their ferocious attack on the body of a dead furred hunter sent him splashing in turn as far and as fast from the dangerous proximity of the feast as he could get.

Rounding a point of the slide, he saw that the smaller pool into which the gash fed its water here joined the lake that had existed earlier, a lake that might, in years or centuries to come, form the sea the flare had steamed from Dis. To swim that, after seeing the carnivorous fish, was impossible. He would have to take the equally dangerous path along under the level rise, where there could be other slips to engulf the luckless.

The rain had almost ceased. The steam grew into a mist, which even the cin-goggles could not penetrate. Nik tightened the strap of the ration pouch and waded on. He had the cliff edge for his guide—and that he could not lose. Eventually, it was going to bring him back to the island hill.

With the waters ankle-high about his fungi-furred boots, he trudged along, wondering if he would ever feel dry again. The fresh dehumidified air of the refuge seemed a dream now. This had been going on for always—lifting a foot, setting it down into oozing sludge, trying to breathe through a water haze—this had been forever and ever, and to it there would be no end.

14

The steam cloaked but did not completely hide the island hill. It was now more truly island than hill, for the lake water had risen to lap about its base. Nik gazed eagerly up at the ledge where he had left Leeds and Vandy. He could see nothing there—they must be lying flat.

Water arose about him as he sloshed to the hill. He moved slowly, worn out by the hours' long push he had made from the reef, suspicious of the footing here. There were signs of the fury of the storm other than just the water. The body of a Disian had been washed between two rocks and floated there face down, rising and falling with the movements of the lake.

A Disian!

Nik splashed on, trying to move faster. If the natives had attacked! He crawled up the slope.

"Leeds! Vandy!" There was no answer to his call.

He had never thought of their not being there, never faced the possibility of coming back to an empty camp. Where had they gone? And why? Had Leeds tried to follow him? But as the captain had pointed out, he could not have made that journey and taken Vandy, too, and certainly the boy could not walk.

"Leeds!" The name came out as a harsh croak as Nik made it over the edge of the ledge.

And the ledge was bare. Bare!

Nik huddled there, too numbed by that discovery to try to think. The storm—! On this exposed position, the storm must have broken with blasting force. Had those

140

two been swept away by wind and water or had the captain somehow made an escape? With that very faint hope moving him, Nik sat back on his heels to look to the next rise of land. The shore cliffs were the only possibility, near enough so that with a determined effort Leeds might have reached them. But what chance had they offered for a semiconscious boy and a man with an injured leg? No, both must have been swept away.

Only stubborn clinging to unrealistic hope made Nik start for the cliffs. There had been plenty of warning about the impending storm, and Leeds knew Dis far better than Nik. The captain must have done *something!* If the cliffs were the only answer, then Leeds had tried the cliffs.

A flock of the leather-winged creatures wheeled over the rocks and screamed as they landed to shamble up and down, eyeing Nik. He gathered they were out to clean up the storm debris. Moving abruptly, Nik was answered by their taking off again with even louder screeches. There were several flocks of them along the cliffs ahead, and some were luckier in their finds, for they settled down to feed.

Had the rugged coast been pounded by the sea that had once filled that basin, Nik could not have made the journey, but the rain lake was waveless, unless purposely disturbed, and shallow, save for a deeper pool now and then. He still walked with caution, but he was trying to move faster.

A glint of light—to his right—from the face of the cliff! Nik waded to that spot. A mass of fungoid brush had been driven into a rock cul-de-sac, and it was from that the wink came. He tore aside the slimy stuff to be faced by a weak torch beam. Perhaps the battering of the storm had affected the charge, for this was only a wan echo of the usual light, but there was no denying that the rod had been carefully wedged into a crevice to provide a guide.

They had reached here alive and with confidence enough to leave a sign for anyone following! Nik had

141

not known how greatly he doubted their safety until relief flooded in to lighten his fear.

And the torch would not have been so carefully set without purpose. He began to search the wall for some other clue, tearing away the matted flotsam with both hands. The last mass of that came free like a released plug, and he was looking into the dark mouth of a cave.

But why—why would Leeds take to such a hole? With the water rising outside, a break in the cliff could be a trap, but Nik was sure this was the road.

He had to stoop to get in, and the torch he had freed from the crevice was very feeble. The light was still strong enough to disclose that this was not a cave, or if it were, the dimensions extended well back into the rock wall.

"Leeds!" he shouted. The name echoed with a hollow, intimidating sound, but there was no other reply.

However, there was another trace of those who had passed this way before him, the shining growing prints of feet that had tracked in crushed plant stuff to the dried floor of the cave. Two sets of those tracks, neither running straight. So Vandy had been on his feet and walking when they entered here! Nik wondered at that minor miracle.

The footprints vanished as their burden of growing slime was shed little by little. But there was only one way they could have gone—straight ahead where the walls closed in to form a passage.

An upslope to the flooring formed a vent in the cliff, angling toward the surface of the shore above. Nik wondered at Leeds' luck in finding it—the perfect bolt hole out of the storm. But with his injured leg, how had the captain made this climb? There were places that were an effort for Nik. He stopped at each and called, certain each time he would be answered—only he never was.

He emerged suddenly into a space he sensed was large but the walls of which he could not see. And standing there, Nik was puzzled. Which way now? To find a wall and work his way around, he decided, was

142

the best answer. The feeble glow of the torch showed him the wall to the right, and he began the journey.

Nik was several feet along before the nature of the wall itself attracted him. This was not rough stone, as were the walls of the cave passage, but smoothly finished with the same coating given to the chambers of the refuge. Here within the sea cliff was another hollowing of the Disians. Another refuge?

There was no cool current of air, just the general dankness of the outside atmosphere, but perhaps not as heavily humid as on the surface. Whatever the purpose of this room, he came across no fixtures, none of the pallid light that had been in the refuge—or had that been added by the Guild?

The size of the chamber was awe-inspiring. Nik was still walking along one wall, the expanse on his left echoing emptily to the sound of his boots on stone. Was this a gallery running within the length of the cliff?

Nik was shivering a little in spite of the humidity. This place did not welcome his kind. For whatever purpose it had been fashioned, those hollowing it had been aliens, and he was not at home here—no off-worlder would be.

"Leeds!" Once more he paused and called. This time the echo came back from all sides until it rang in his head almost as that throbbing whistle had done.

But there had been an answer! A cry that was not a real word but that echoed in turn, so that he was certain he had heard it, if not what it was.

"Vandy!" Nik faced outward into that unknown space to his left and put the full force of his lungs into that shout.

This time no answer came. He tried to think where the earlier sound had come from, but the echoes made that impossible. To strike out from the wall was dangerous. He could only keep on exploring with that as his guide. But there was a need for hurry, and Nik began to trot.

A few moments brought him to a corner and the angle of another wall to follow. This was broken by slits, which had been filled in, perhaps at a later time, with rough stones wedged and mortared together. Windows walled up? Exits closed against some peril?

His torch caught and held in one that was a dark gap, not sealed. Nik hesitated. A way out—or *the* way out?

He listened. Now that the faint echo of his own footfalls had died, was there anything to hear? Just as he had been alerted to the Disian ambush by those lights, so now he was uneasy because of the very silence about him. His imagination pictured only too readily something lurking there—waiting. For what? For Nik Kolherne to come within attacking distance?

The dim torch flashed within the wall cavity, giving him nothing save the assurance that it was more than a niche, an entrance to either a passage or another room. He could not stay here forever—he must either take that door or continue his wall-hugging advance. And something he could not define urged him into the passage. After all, he could always return—

There was an oppression here that he connected with the humid air but that carried with it a dampening to more than just the physical senses—an oppression of spirits as well as of body. Why had he suddenly thought of it that way? Men—or at least intelligent entities—had made this place for a purpose, the desperate purpose of a refuge? Or had this existed before the time when the Disians had foreseen their world's end and tried to last out catastrophe and chaos?

Nik went one step at a time, pausing to listen for that odd cry, for sounds of movement that might mean he was being stalked. His imagination could provide more than one answer, but still he crept on.

This was not another room but a lengthening passage, so narrow his shoulders brushed the walls. Nik began to count the paces, ten, twelve— Now the outline of another door was visible.

More than an outline, there was light ahead—the outer day? But Nik came out into another chamber

144

where the alien quality of his surroundings reached a peak.

Reptilian life! He almost drew his blaster—until he saw that those rounded lengths were not legless bodies but roots—or branches—of plants. They stretched across the floor, tangled and intertwined, but they all reached for a crack in the middle through which flowed a stream of water. The roots were outsize, the plants they nourished relatively small, forming a line of white fleshy growths along the walls. And from them arose a musty odor, adding to the heaviness of the air.

"Welcome back!"

Nik started. He had been so intent upon that loathsome growth that he had not seen the man within the arch of roots until Leeds spoke.

"How—" Nik stepped over a hump of root, somehow shrinking from any contact with the growth. "Vandy?" he demanded before he completed his first question.

"All right. You're alone? You didn't get the rations?"

Leeds' eyes were deep in his head; his face was fined down until the bony ridges of cheekbones and chin were too clearly defined. He did not move as Nik came up.

Leeds' eyes—his goggles were gone! The light from the unearthly plants must give him a measure of sight, but what had happened to his cins? Nik bestrode another root tangle and was at Leeds' side.

The captain's injured leg was stretched stiffly out, tightly bound to a length of thick plant stem, the end of which protruded beyond his boot sole and was splintered and worn.

"I take it the storm's over," he said wearily.

"Yes." Nik looked for Vandy, but the boy was nowhere in sight.

He shifted the strap of the ration bag from his shoulder and dumped the pouch beside Leeds. "Here're the rations. Where's Vandy?"

Leeds grimaced. "An answer I wish I could give you—"

Nik stooped to catch the other's shoulder. "What do you mean?"

"Just that. No, you fool, I didn't leave him behind or knock him out or do any of those things you're thinking! Why should I? He's our only pass out of here. That's why you have to find him."

"Find him! But what happened?"

"I had a packet of Sustain tablets." Leeds' voice was very tired. "Thought about them later and gave them to him—they brought him around all right. Then, we saw the storm coming and knew we had to move. He didn't want to go—had a tussle with him—but without goggles he didn't want to stay alone either. We went along the cliffs and found this hole. But it was a long trip in this far with my leg bad. By the time we reached here, I was pretty tired. Then the boy took over."

"Took over—how?"

Leeds' mirthless grin was a wider stretch of tight skin and thin lips. "By knocking me out, taking the goggles, and going on his own. There's no way of telling how long he's had to set distance between us. But he's gone—somewhere. And you're the only one who can track him—unless you *did* bring the Patrol. And that wouldn't be good for us under the circumstances. He has both blasters, too—at least mine's gone!"

"But why—" Part of this Nik thought he could understand—the taking of Leeds' goggles, yes. To be eternally in the dark on this hostile world would have led an older man to make such an attempt much sooner, but to strike out alone—Vandy, though, had once before played just such a trick on him back in the ruined city.

"He's conditioned," Leeds said flatly. "He'd stay with you but not with me. I thought he would be easy to handle—as soon as he got energy enough, he made a run for it. And I needn't remind you, Kolherne, that if the Patrol does catch up with us and he isn't here— This bag—did you go all the way to the refuge?"

"No, they found me. I was with them coming here when the storm hit." Nik remembered Commander

146

i'Inad. Yes, Leeds was entirely right. If the Patrol caught up with them now and Vandy was missing, they would suffer for it. There was no evidence that they ever had the boy at all. They *had* to find Vandy with the cins and maybe two blasters, urged by his conditioning to put as much distance between Leeds and himself as he could—where would he go?

"You were here when he jumped you?" he demanded.

"Yes. A good thing for me. These plant things give off some light. If he'd left me in the dark with this leg—"

"And you don't know how long ago?"

"All I know is that I sat down to ease my leg. The next thing I remember, I was lying on my back with a big ache behind my eyes. And I'm not even sure how long ago that was."

"You'd better eat." Nik took one of the ration containers out of the pouch and handed it to Leeds. "Any other way out of this place except that passage? And does he have a torch?"

"No, we left that as a signal—which I see you found."

No torch. Even with the cins on, to retreat along that passage and into the big chamber was a move Nik would not care to make. But had Vandy been driven hard enough by his conditioning to do just that? He'd have a look around here first.

Leeds pressed the button on the container. The hands with which he held the tin were shaking. Nik gazed about the root-matted room. At the opposite end of the room, there was one easily noticed exit, the way the water flowed, and that was large enough for a stooping man to enter. Vandy could have walked through there. Nik went to inspect that exit.

He noted that any touching of the roots left dark bruises on their surfaces—one way of tracing Vandy's passage. But those clustered at the mouth of the water tunnel were unmarked. Either they had recovered in that interval of time between Vandy's flight and now or he had not tried that path.

Nik began a circuit of the walls. The plants were

147

more thickly massed to the left; to the right only a few smaller and more widely spaced ones grew. The entrance to this whole series of cavern rooms had been hidden behind a plug of vegetation. Could another such exist here behind the plants? He loathed going near them, but it had to be done.

Only, as far as he could see, there was no break in the wall behind them, and the light given off by their fleshy leaves, those twining reptilian roots, was enough to make the rock surfaces plainly visible. It began to appear that Vandy had gone back down the entrance passage. Nik said as much, but the captain shook his head.

"Without a torch—no. He hated that place when we came through, dragged back on me all the way. That's what made me so tired that I got careless when I hit here and he stopped whining about being in the dark. The cins wouldn't give him vision enough there. He went some other way. Through that water channel probably—"

Nik went back to the channel. He did not see how even one as slight as Vandy could have worked his way through the mass of roots directly before that opening without leaving some trace on the vegetation. The marks of his own passing were not only darkened, but now, a few moments after that bruising, the stuff seemed to be sloughing off as if his touch had killed it. Vandy's path had to be the other way—in spite of Leeds' report.

The captain had finished the contents of the container. "Think the Patrol will follow you?"

Remembering Commander i'Inad, Nik had no doubt of that. But whether the Patrol could trace him into this cave maze, he did not know.

Leeds had been fingering the pouch; now he looked up with a very grim twist of lips.

"Well, I do!" he said. "Look here."

He turned the pouch upside down, sending its contents spinning and displaying to Nik the inner part. There was a small bar set there.

148

"Caster!" Leeds identified. "They probably have had a fix on this all the time. Any supply pouch taken would lead them right to us. They obviously foresaw a jump try on your part."

"So, the Patrol could be on the way even now, coming up the passage, and with Vandy gone—"

The goggles must not have masked his face too much for Leeds to read his expression, for the captain nodded again.

"Just so—they will be coming. And our answer is Vandy. So we'd better find him—and quick!"

15

Nik fingered the supply bag, staring down at the telltale rod. The Patrol would have a fix on that all right. Maybe Barketh had deliberately set him up this way, allowing an escape at the first opportunity so they could trace him and then claim the bargain off—but they were not here yet. Methodically, he began to twist and wad the pouch into as small a compass as possible. Now he and Leeds needed time. Finding this had changed his plan for trailing Vandy. He could not leave the captain here alone to be picked up by the Patrol with no Vandy. Commander i'Inad might just burn him out of hand.

"What are you doing?" Leeds wanted to know.

"Giving them something to follow." Nik went back to the stream exit from the root chamber. He was certain now Vandy had not gone that way, but something smaller and more dangerous to them could. Nik thrust the supply bag between two of the curling roots into the water, where the current of the stream, weak though it was, tugged the container out of sight. The Patrol fix was on the move again, and Nik thought that any tracker might have a rather difficult time following it along its present path.

"That makes sense." Leeds applauded his action. "But they'll come this far—" He pulled himself up a little as if to test his ability to get to his feet.

"Yes, so we'll be gone," Nik answered. "Only we have to pick the right road." He went back to his survey of the chamber walls. Vandy had left here, and Leeds

150

seemed very sure the boy had not backtracked on the way in. Then there was another way out, and, taking it, he must have left some trace for Nik to find.

"I'm not exactly up to a clean lift out of here," the captain commented. He was standing, or rather leaning, braced among the roots. "You can't blast off at a good rate with me slowing the rockets, and back there I'm lost without goggles." He spoke levelly, not as if he were trying to ask for assistance but as one merely pointing out the disadvantages of some proposed plan. Neither did he offer any suggestions.

"Vandy got out of here some way!" Nik's frustration at not finding any trail was rising to something stronger than irritation. By all he could discover, Vandy had simply vanished into thin air—unless Leeds was wrong and Vandy *had* backtracked.

"He *must* have gone back!" he added, but the captain shook his head.

"You don't know how hard it was to get him through there the first time. I had to drag him. He kept saying there was something there waiting to get us—"

"He has the goggles now—" Nik was beginning, but the memory of that sensation he himself had felt, that there was something he could not see or hear lurking, ready and waiting for him to step beyond some intangible barrier of safety, came back to him.

"Even the goggles aren't much use without a torch there. I know they weren't for me. We were really lucky to get this far."

Nik moved on along the wall. There was another exit here then, somewhere. And it was the susceptibility of the roots to touch that finally revealed it. A blackened, withering length caught his eye, and he hurried to it. Vandy must have set foot there to climb to the opening above. Nik regarded the hole with a measuring eye. It was small but not too small, he thought, for both of them to squeeze through. Yet what if they found the going on the other side rough—with Leeds crippled. On the other hand, could he leave the captain behind now with the Patrol following the fix?

"So that's the way!" Leeds hobbled across to join Nik, his step a sidewise lurch and recover, which drew lines about his mouth and tightened his lips.

"Can you make it up there?"

"It's a matter of have to now, isn't it?" the captain returned. "We never know just what we can do until we have to. Give us a hand now—"

Somehow with Leeds' straining to lift himself and Nik's boosting, the captain made it up to the hole. He clung there to look down.

"Better get those supplies—" He nodded at the tins beside the stream. "If we do catch up with that brat, we'll need them."

Nik shed his damp tunic, bundled the containers into it, and so fashioned a pack. How long *could* Vandy keep going on the Sustain pills? It might be that they would find him exhausted not too far ahead. He scrambled up to join Leeds.

"You'll have to be eyes for both of us from now on." The captain hooked his fingers in Nik's belt. "And I'm not up to either a fast run or an easy climb. But let's take off—"

Nik had to keep the dying torch for emergencies and depend upon the goggles. But in this crack, as they drew away from the ghostly glimmer of the root room, he was almost as blind as Leeds. And they must go so slowly, a crippled fumbling, when he was goaded by the need for haste.

Luckily, the footing here was even, so regular that Nik thought it had been purposely smoothed. This was no natural fissure in the rock but an established passage. Also, there was a distinct current of air, not quite as humid as that of the outer surface. Could they be heading into another refuge?

There were tenuous traces of Vandy here. The footprints where he had left some vegetable deposits from the roots made faint marks on the flooring, but these dwindled, to vanish entirely.

"Listen!"

Nik did not need that alert from Leeds. Far away or

else distorted by the walls of the winding passage—there was no mistaking that whistle that hurt the ears and was a throb within the skull. Nik took a longer stride forward, and Leeds went off balance, stumbling into him and bringing them both up against the supporting wall.

"Keep on course!" the captain snapped. "What is it?"

"The Disians! They hunted me on the way back; now they must be after Vandy!"

"What Disians?" Leeds demanded. When Nik told him, he whistled in turn, but not the throbbing call of the natives.

"We never saw any of them! Men here—natives?"

"Not much like men now." Nik corrected grimly. "They're hunters and they hunt for—food—"

Vandy in the dark, being hunted as Nik had been—watched, driven, finally lured into the open. There, at the last, in spite of Nik's off-world weapon and determination to stand up to danger, the primitives had brought him out as an easy kill. And if they could do that to him, forewarned and armed, what would they do to Vandy!

"We have to get to him!" Nik burst out. He caught at Leeds' arm, pulled the captain close enough to support him, and then pushed them both on. Leeds made no complaint, but Nik could hear the panting breaths the other drew and guessed that the captain was straining his powers to the limit. Yet they still kept to a short-paced shuffle.

Just that one whistle. They did not hear another, although Nik listened not only with his ears, it seemed, but also with every nerve in his tiring body. Had that been the signal to begin a hunt, not to urge attack? Suppose they came up from the rear and caught the Disians from behind? Vandy was armed. After his experience in the ruins and on the reef, the boy would be alert against dangers native to Dis and the dark. Whether that would give him a small measure of safety now, Nik did not know. He could not do more than hope.

"Light—" Leeds got the word out between two gasping breaths.

It was very faint that light, but it was there. They headed for it and came out in another large chamber.

"Refuge!" Leeds cried.

The walls had a glow that did not extend far down the passage. It was as if some invisible curtain hung there.

"It's bright—"

"Not to me. That's what the goggles do for you," Leeds commented. "But it is like refuge light all right. We stepped this up back at the base after we took over."

"But this can't be the same refuge," Nik protested. "We're a long way from there."

"Maybe it's not the same series of burrows but another system. Or it could be the same. We never did explore a lot of the tunnels—no reason to. We just closed off those we didn't need."

"You can see here." Nik took in the possibilities of that. He thought, observing Leeds, that the captain would not be able to keep on his feet much longer.

"Yes, I can see." Leeds' tone was colorless, neither adding to nor denying that fact. "All right—you go on. Let me follow at my own pace."

The decision was the only one that made good sense. If the Disians were hunting Vandy somewhere in this maze, Nik had to find him before they closed in. And Leeds was close to collapse.

"Give me a couple of the supply tins—and your blaster and the torch," the captain continued. He had reached the wall of a room and was lowering himself with it as a steadying brace.

The supplies—yes, Nik would leave some of those. And the torch. It was nearly exhausted now. But the blaster—with Vandy ahead in danger? Nik had to weigh one demand against the other. He opened the tunic bundle and took out two of the containers. Now as he tied up the roll again, he said flatly, "I can't give you the blaster. The Disians are hunting."

"And if they double back here?" Leeds asked just as tonelessly. "The boy has two weapons—and you have that." He pointed to the fringe of mock tools and fantastic arms that were part of Hacon's equipment.

"Those? You know they're fakes!"

"Fakes maybe for the uses Vandy dreamed for them, but they could have other uses—"

Leeds was not so far wrong, Nik thought. He had used one of those gadgets to force open the armory door back at the refuge. But that any of them could be a practical weapon against Disian attack, he doubted.

"That one—" The captain pointed at the one that in some manner resembled a blaster. In Vandy's fantasy, it shot a ray that turned its victims into stone. Nik only wished that the property with which Vandy had endowed that hunk of metal were a true one.

"Have you tried it?" Leeds continued.

"It doesn't work." Nik wondered if Leeds' mind was affected by his exertions.

"Maybe not the way Vandy intended. But we gave you some fireworks to use to impress, and that is one of them. Try it."

Nik drew the weapon. It was lighter than the blaster, of course, a small, bright toy. Now he aimed it at a midpoint of the chamber and pressed the firing button.

A second later he cried out, his hand sweeping up to cover his goggled eyes. The answering burst of light had been blinding!

"Take off your goggles now," Leeds ordered.

Nik obeyed. Blinking, he looked out into the chamber. There was light there, but not blinding any more.

"To infrared based sight, that burst is blinding," the captain told him. "And the effect lingers for some moments, long enough for you to make some attack. Creech thought that one up, and he's a com-tech with real brains."

"Why didn't you tell me about it before?" Nik wanted to know. Back there in the ruins when Vandy had been surrounded by the furred hunters or later—when he had fallen prey to the lure of the Disians—he could have used this.

Leeds met his accusing stare unruffled. "I told you that I believe in luck. I didn't expect you to have to take off here on Dis but to stay put in the refuge. And—it's well to have some insurance. There was a chance, of course, that you'd discover its use, but there was also a chance we might have been put in a position to need a new weapon, just as we are. Nobody but Creech and I knew that rayer was more than a prop for Hacon the hero. And it's always well to nurse a star in reserve while you're moving your comet on the broad swoop. Orkhad came in on this deal against my wishes. I had to foresee the possibility of a showdown—"

Nik understood. This all fitted with Leeds as he had learned to know him.

"And if we were disarmed, they wouldn't suspect this tinware?" Nik flipped a finger along the fake equipment.

"Just so. But you have a weapon now, and I need the blaster."

Nik drew the more conventional weapon and weighed them both in his hands as he considered the point. The rayer was a weapon, right enough. But on the other hand, he was sure of the effect of the blaster.

"Make up your mind!" That was sharp. "You haven't too long—for more than one reason—"

"Yes, the Patrol and the Disians." Nik rehooked the rayer, but he still turned the blaster over in hesitant fingers.

"And a third—you haven't looked in a mirror lately!"

"Mirror?" Nik repeated. Then his right hand went to his face fearfully. He was afraid to brush fingers across cheek and jaw.

"Without your goggles"—Leeds was matter of fact—"it's beginning to show. Gyna was right in her doubts of full success. I don't know the rate of slip, but if you don't catch up with Vandy soon, you may not be able to play Hacon when you do. And if you front him as Nik

156

Kolherne, I don't think you'll have any influence over him."

Under those questing fingertips, the skin did feel rough! How long—hours? A day? Maybe two before it really began to break and return him to the horror from which a small boy would shrink.

Nik was cold, shaking. He had to brace himself to keep on his feet. The blaster—there was one way he could end the nightmare—with the blaster.

But Leeds now moved with a speed and precision that Nik thought he had lost. His arm shot out, the edge of his hand chopped Nik's wrist, and the blaster fell between them, with Leeds scooping it up.

"I would advise you to go—and fast!" All the crack of an order was in that. "We have to get Vandy out of here. And if you ever want a human face again, you'll get him! Just to make sure you'll hunt him, I'll keep this—"

He held the blaster on the knee of his good leg, looking up at Nik with such complete belief in himself that it was as strong as a blow. Because Nik had been Hacon for so long without thinking of the change that might come, to return now to that other would be worse than he dared to consider. Pulling the bundle of supplies up under his arm, he did not even look back at Leeds as he staggered across the chamber to the opening on the far side, his hand to his cheek.

As he went through that doorway, Nik forced his fingers away, his arm down to his side. He did not want to know—he did not dare to learn how bad it was. Leeds was right as always. Nik had to find Vandy before he ceased to be Hacon and so lost all control over the boy. He had to find Vandy to buy his own future, his chance to be a man in the company of his kind.

For a space, he trudged on mechanically, all his thoughts turned inward, the chill of fear still riding him. Then he forced both thoughts and fears back and centered his attention on the task at hand. There had been only one way into that back chamber, and Vandy had taken it. There was only one way out—along here.

157

Nik snapped his goggles back into place, trying hard not to touch his face too much in the process. Instantly the walls glowed with a light as bright as any in the Dipple rooms—but he wasn't going to think of the Dipple and Korwar!

There was no trace of footprints on the floor of the passage, no break in the glowing walls. But there was— Nik lifted his head and expanded his nostrils, striving to catch that elusive scent. Yes—the sickly odor of vegetation! Either this passage ran on to the outside or to another root room. The current of air was blowing straight into his face, and it carried the smell.

No sound. Nik longed to shout for Vandy. Whether the boy would either pause or listen, or whether the noise might bring the other lurkers out of the burrows to him, he could not tell, but both risks were too great. He was trotting now, the bundle of supplies swinging and bumping against his hip, intent on beating time itself.

The corridor made an angled turn, and Nik found his opening to the outside, a break in the wall there where part of the cliff face must long ago have given way. But it was no door; the drop from the cut was a sheer one, past any descending.

Nik edged past that point and caught his first sign of the fugitive, a boot print in the soil the wind had drifted in the cut. Vandy had been this way, but how long ago? No other marks except that. If he had been the quarry in some chase, the pursuers had left no traces of their own passing.

It seemed to Nik that the walls were less bright, that their glow was fading. And then there was an abrupt change from light to dark, as if whatever principle kept up the age-old illumination of the refuge had here failed or shorted.

There—that sensation of watchful waiting just beyond! Nik paused. He was so very sure he was not alone that he wet his lips preparatory to calling Vandy.

What kept him silent was perhaps some instinct for preservation he was not aware of possessing.

Light again—about chest high in the middle of the passage—stationary. No off-world torch, nothing he could understand. It did not spread to illuminate the walls, the floor, the roof above it—it simply was a patch of light seemingly born of the air without power to throw its beam.

Nik studied it with growing uneasiness. For a long moment, it was there, a bright dot in the dark. Then it began to move, not toward him, not in retreat, but up and down, side to side, in a series of sharply defined swings.

A lure—a Disian lure!

He backed away toward the lighted part of the passage and the break in the wall. If they were going to rush him, he wanted light for the battle. But the lure did not follow. He stopped again.

If it was a trap, it was one he had to dare. Vandy had taken this road. In order to find Vandy, he would have to travel it, too. The trap and the lure—with a blaster he could have burned the road open, but Leeds had the blaster. The rayer—could light save him here?

Nik slipped up the goggles, bringing the world about him into deep dusk. Instantly he realized he had made the right choice. There was a second glow ahead beside the lure—which he saw now only as if it were a tiny spark at the end of a long tunnel. This was an aura outlining something that squatted low beneath the lure, supplying the bait and perhaps the trap in one.

Once more he began to advance with the rayer in his hand. He aimed. The lure danced in a wilder swing, and Nik fired.

16

What must have been an eye-searing burst to goggled eyes was bearable to Nik's naked sight. There was a shrill, thin screeching, which hurt his ears and his head as had the throb whistles of the Disians. That blotch of creature on the floor reared, throwing up and out long jointed legs, to crack and contract, until it toppled over and lay on its back kicking.

The light lingered as if the ray had ignited particles in the air. And now by its aid, Nik saw the other—one of the naked humanoids crouched behind its hound, if the jointed thing could be so termed. The Disian writhed, hands over his eyes.

Nik ran forward, This was his only chance, and he had to take advantage of it. The wriggling thing on the ground had stopped kicking, one of its clawed feet remaining straight up in the air. But there was space to pass that recumbent form.

He made that passage in a leap. The upright leg swung and struck Nik across the upper arm with such force that he staggered, but forward and not against the wall. The thing was scrabbling wildly, striving to turn over on its feet once again, squealing loudly as it struggled, to be answered with one of those whistles from its humanoid companion.

Nik faced around. The fiery light was dying. While the kicker still lay supine, the Disian was on his feet, shading his eyes but fronting the off-worlder. He had the stance of one ready to carry on the fight.

For the second time, Nik fired the rayer and then

turned and ran, his heart pounding, the bundle of supplies knocking painfully against him at every step. He snapped down the goggles again, and instantly the glare behind him was a warning of the force he had loosed to pin his enemies fast. He might have been able to blind, to immobilize them for a space, but he had not gagged them, and the din behind was now a torment in his head, a mingling of the squealing and the whistle. Nik had no doubt that help was being summoned and he might meet it on its way.

The dark walls continued, and he held to the hope that any Disians answering that summons would betray themselves by their body glow, as had those who had set up the ambush without. He had to slow his pace. He could not keep running in the thick air of this burrow. His breaths were sobs that raised and racked his ribs and set a knife thrust of pain in his side.

Behind him, a little of the glare still existed. Perhaps a second dose had effectively removed the clawed thing from the field. It had taken the full force of the first raying and had been unprotected at the second. At least its squeal sounded more faintly, and Nik believed it had not stirred from the place where it fell. The Disian was another matter—the whistling had quieted. Did that mean that whatever message the native had striven to give was at an end? Or had he fallen silent because he was stalking Nik?

Twice the off-worlder paused to look back. There was the glow, but against it he could sight no moving thing. Only he could not be sure on such slight evidence that he was *not* trailed.

Light ahead again, another section where the walls still held their radiance. The small portion of dark before that was a logical place for an ambush. Nik studied the walls, the floor—not a glimmer of body glow. He had a feeling that if he could reach the lighted portion, he would be safe for the present.

Once more he forced his body to a trot, his hand pressed tight against his side. The effort exhausted him so much that he was frightened. That booster drink Barketh had given him back at the refuge—were the effects of it now wearing off? Would the need for rest and nourishment lead to his defeat? There was no place here where he would dare to stop for either.

Nik was tottering when he came into the light and had to lean against the wall, his shoulders flat on its surface, as he looked up and down the passage. Far back in the dark, there was still a shimmer of glow, the residue of the ray. Ahead, not too far away, the corridor made another turn, masking its length beyond. Nik tired to control his gusty breathing and to listen. The squealing had stopped; there was no more whistling. He could hear nothing from behind or beyond.

He edged along the wall, watching both ways as best he could. Had Vandy fallen into just such a trap as had faced Nik—and was he now in the hands of the Disians?

Nik reached the turn in the corridor, got around it, and saw before him a wide space giving opening to a score of passages, another terminal such as they had seen in the refuge. He sagged back hopelessly against the wall. To explore every one of those was beyond his strength or ability now. Only a guess could guide him. Vandy, if he had reached this point, would have been moved only by chance.

He also knew that he was almost at the end of whatever strength the booster had supplied. How long had it been since he had left the refuge in the company of the Patrol squad? More than a full Disian day, Nik was sure—perhaps even two. He squatted down, his back to the wall, at a point from which he could view at a glance all those empty tunnel mouths, and tried to think. The bundle of supply containers was under his hand, and he ached with the need for food. Just one of those— He had to have its contents inside him or he might never be able to drag on past this halt.

Reluctantly Nik took out a container and triggered its heat and open button. He ate the contents slowly, making each mouthful last as long as he could. As with all emergency supplies, this had a portion of sustainer included. The warmth and savor of the concentrated food settled into him, and he relaxed in spite of the need for vigilance. Food—rest—he dared the former but not the latter!

Five doorways before him, five chances of finding Vandy, and he had hardly time to take one—one—one—

It was dark and he was running through the dark, while behind him padded a hunting pack, the furred creatures from the ruins, the bare-skinned Disians and their insectival hounds—after him—after him!

Nik gave a stifled cry and strove to throw himself forward, out from under the grasping hands, the claws, the bared fangs—

His head, it hurt— He opened his eyes—into dark!

Dark! His hands went to his goggles, but there were no goggles! Frantically he felt for the cord at his neck—he must have fallen asleep and scraped them off somehow. But they were not there, hanging on his chest! He felt about him in the dark—carefully at first and then more wildly—but they were totally gone.

"I have them!"

Nik stiffened. "Vandy?" he asked, though he had to wet his lips to make them frame that name. "Vandy?" he repeated with rising inflection when there came no answer. He had thought a measure of subdued light might linger here as it had in the chamber where he had left Leeds, but perhaps this glow was different, for without the goggles he was in a dusk so thick that he might as well have been blind. He thought he could hear hurried breathing to his right.

"Vandy!" That was a demand for an answer.

"You aren't Hacon. There never was a real Hacon—"

Nik tried to think clearly. Hacon—what had that to do with the here and now? No, this was not one of Vandy's heroic adventures; this was very real and dangerous.

"*You* aren't real," that voice out of the dark continued. "You're one of them!" That was accusation rather than identification.

It was so hard to think. Nik must have been asleep when Vandy found him and took the goggles. How was he going to argue with the boy? He still felt dazed from that sudden awakening.

What had Leeds said back there? That the change in his face had already begun. No wonder, when he had taken the goggles, that Vandy had decided Nik was not Hacon. Nik's hand went to his face in the old masking gesture.

"You're one of them," Vandy repeated. "I can just leave you here in the dark. Like that captain—he was one of them, too!"

"One of whom, Vandy?" Somehow Nik was able to ask that.

"One of those who want my father to give up the stronghold. I'm going now—"

"Vandy!" All Nik's panic was in that. He fought back to a measure of self-control and asked, "Where are you going?"

"Out. I know that the Patrol are here. They'll find me—I can call them. Now I have supplies and blasters and goggles—" His voice was growing fainter. Nik caught a scrape of boot on rock—to the left this time.

His control broke. "Vandy!" He threw himself after the sound of those withdrawing footsteps and crashed against a wall. There was the patter of running. Vandy must have entered one of the tunnels. Nik sucked in his breath, steadied himself, and fought a terrible battle with insane panic. He was alone, without goggles, and Vandy had taken the supply bundle also—

He had two choices—to go back, to try and reach the chamber where he had left Leeds, which meant passing through the section where the Disian had laid the trap, or to trace Vandy on through the maze where he was a blind man. Which?

Nik was certain that Vandy had taken the passage farthest to his left. Trying to recall the terminal as he had seen it last, he believed he could find that opening. And the boy could not run far in this humid air. Sooner or later he would have to rest. Nik must follow him. To return through the Disian trap was more than he could force himself to try. He stretched out his arms and

164

began to feel his way along the wall against which he had crashed. Seconds later, his right hand went into open space, and he knew he had found his doorway.

The weapon against fear was concentration, concentration upon what he was doing, upon sounds. Nik's senses of hearing and touch had to serve him now in place of sight. Fingers running along the rock surface to his left were his guides, leaving his right hand free for the rayer. And he tried to make his own footfalls as quiet as possible, so that he could listen with all his might.

Footfalls, far less cautious than his own, were ahead! Nik knew a sudden rush of excitement, so that he had to will himself to keep his own cautious rate of advance. He had been right. The run that had taken Vandy away from him had slowed quickly to a walk, which was hardly faster than his own creep. But—the boy could *see!* Let Vandy turn his head and he would sight Nik, and he had the blasters! An alarm could make Vandy use one of those almost as a reflex action. So much depended upon chance now—the chance that Vandy would not look behind him—the greater chance that Nik must take in trying to reason with the scared boy.

Vandy had thrown aside Hacon and the fantasy that had let him accept Nik, and he was conditioned against strangers. This meant that conditioning would now act against Nik and any contact he might try to make.

But every inch Nik covered with those footfalls still steady before him strengthened his belief in himself, stilled his first panic. It almost sounded as if Vandy knew where he was going and had some clue as to what lay ahead—not that that could be true!

Then the footfalls ceased. Nik backed against the wall. He was a small target in that position but one that could not escape blaster fire. He waited as weakness flooded through his body. Not to be able to see—

No sound, no sound at all. Vandy must be watching him—getting ready to fire? Nik ached with the effort to make his ears serve him as eyes.

Perhaps it was that very intensity of effort that sharpened Nik's thinking. He had been wrong in his handling of Vandy back there; he was certain of that now. At least he could try to repair the damage.

"Vandy!" He made that into a demand for attention, not an appeal. "Have the Fannards taken you over?"

Again he strained to hear. Because he had known that he was not Hacon, he had tamely accepted Vandy's recognition of that fact. But he had been thinking then as himself, Nik Kolherne, and not as Vandy. To Vandy, the fantasy world that had been Hacon's had been so real that he had accepted the appearance of its major inhabitant in the flesh as a perfectly normal happening. He could doubt Hacon's identity now, but there should be some residue of belief to make him doubt that doubt in turn. And if Nik could push him back into the fantasy, even for a short space, he could re-establish contact.

"Have they, Vandy?" He raised his voice and heard the faint echo of it. His face—had it been the change in his face that had set Vandy off? Again his searching fingers advised him of a slight roughness, but not the spongy softness he had feared to touch—not yet.

"There're no Fannards here." The reply was sullen, suspicious.

"How do you know, Vandy?" Nik pressed that slight advantage. At least the boy had answered him. "They can't be seen, even with goggles—you know that."

The Fannards—those invisible entities Vandy had produced for menace in one of the Hacon adventures. In this place, one *could* believe in them. Nik could—

He heard the click of boot plates, not away this time but toward him. Once more that sound stopped, but he was sure Vandy stood not too far away watching him. Nik spoke again.

"There are hunters here." He kept his voice casual, as much what Hacon's should be as he could. Hacon was Vandy's superman. Nik must reproduce a Hacon now or complete the boy's disillusionment and proba-

166

bly doom the both of them. "They set a trap back there, but I got through—"

"There aren't any Fannards!" Vandy proclaimed loudly. "You aren't Hacon either!"

"Are you sure, Vandy?" Nik made himself keep calm and held his voice level. *He* was sure of only one thing. Vandy had come closer; he had not withdrawn yet. "We are being hunted, Vandy. And I am Hacon!" In a way he was—perhaps not the superman Vandy had created, but he was a companion in danger, devoted now to bring the boy out of that same danger. And so he was Hacon, no matter what his ravaged face might argue.

"No Fannards—" Vandy repeated stubbornly. But again the boot plates tapped out an encouraging message for Nik's ears. "This isn't the Gorge of Tath either!"

"No these are the Burrows of Dis, but still we are hunted. Vandy, do you know the way out of here?"

There was a long moment of silence, and then the boy answered in a low voice.

"No."

"Neither do I," Nik told him. "But we have to find one—before we're found. And the hunt is up behind—"

"I know." But Vandy came no closer. Nik did not know how much acceptance he had won, but he plunged.

"Why did you take this passage?"

"It was the nearest. Two of the others just end in rooms—no way out."

"What about it—do we go together?"

"Here—" Something flipped through the dark, struck against Nik's chest, and was gone before he could raise his hand to grasp it.

"On the floor, by your right foot." Vandy's direction came with cool assurance.

It was difficult to remember that what was dark to him was light for the begoggled boy. Nik went down on one knee and groped until his fingers closed about a piece of stuff that could have been a dried root or vine.

"What—" he began when Vandy interrupted him.

"I say the Fannards have taken *you* over. You're

167

Hacon, but it's my sotry—always *my* story—and we are in it."

Nik felt the cord tighten; Vandy held the other end. Should he give that tie a jerk, try to get the boy within reach? But such an aggression on his part would break the thin bond of trust. He was impressed by the shrewdness of Vandy's reasoning. If Nik had endeavored to push them back into the fantasy, then Vandy would play—by the original rules. The adventures of Hacon had been created by Vandy and would continue so. That the boy had made the switch was the surprising part. His flight from Leeds might have been triggered by his conditioning and suspicion, but his ability to get this far, to remain reasonably steady in the whole wild Disian adventure, would have been more believable had he continued to think himself in some Hacon-Vandy adventure. Instead, he knew this was real and yet had not yielded to fright or panic. This suggested he was tough-fibered and determined.

There was nothing to do now but to go ahead with the game on Vandy's terms and try to win back to the Hacon-leader pattern, which the boy had earlier allowed. Nik gave the cord a twist about his wrist and the slightest of tugs to make sure his guess was right—that Vandy intended to lead him now. The cord held.

"There is only one way to go," Nik remarked. "They must be ahead of us—perhaps waiting all through these burrows. We'll have to go back. The Patrol will come in that way." Nik hastened to pile up arguments that might influence the boy. "They were with me until we were caught in a storm, and I lost touch—"

He stared into the dark. Vandy was watching him—he must be! And Nik's tone of voice and his expression were the only ways he had to influence the other.

There was a small sound, not quite a laugh, but it held a note of derision. Again Nik was disconcerted. Vandy was a boy, a small boy, someone to be led, protected, guided. The Vandy he met here in the dark was far too mature and able.

168

"So we go back? I thought you said they had traps there?" The amusement in that was not childlike.

Nik kept to the exact truth. "They do—I broke through one. But you have two blasters—"

"No, I used one up."

Was that the truth? Nik swallowed and began again. "There is still one—and the Disians give themselves away."

"How?"

"With the lures." Nik explained about the swinging lights and the aura given off by Disian bodies.

"Then you don't mean the worm things?" For the first time, Vandy sounded less assured and really puzzled.

"Worm things?"

"They light up when you step near their holes. There were a lot of them in one of the passages. That's where I used up the blaster. But I never saw these other things. This is for true?"

Again he was separating the real from the fantasy, and at the risk of losing contact, Nik kept to the truth.

"This is for real—just as your worm things were for real."

"All right. But to go back there—"

"To go on," Nik pointed out patiently, "is maybe to tangle with something even a blaster can't handle, Vandy. And the Patrol are behind." He took a bigger chance. "This is your story, Vandy, but it has to work out to the right end, doesn't it? Give me my goggles—"

The rope suddenly went lax, and Nik knew he had erred.

"No!" Vandy's response was emphatic. "I keep the goggles. I keep this blaster. If you want to come along, all right—but this is my story, and we're going my way."

The cord tightened once again, pulling Nik forward. For the moment he had lost. He accepted that—but only for the moment.

17

It was one of the most difficult things Nik had ever done to allow Vandy to tow him along through the dark. As he followed the tugs of the cord linking them, he tried to plan, to think of some way of regaining Vandy's cooperation.

"Vandy, are you hungry?" Nik made his first attempt on the level he thought might be easiest.

"I ate—while you slept back there!" Again that oddly adult amusement in the reply.

"Good." Nik felt that he must keep talking, that words could unite them better than the cord. "Vandy, you have the goggles. What do you see now?"

The boy seemed to consider that deserving of an answer.

"Just walls lighted up a little—not as much as back there, though."

"No openings in them?" Nik persisted. The possibility of another ambush was always in his mind.

"No—" Vandy began and then corrected himself as the twitch on the cord became a jerk. "There's a door—up there. And—"

But Nik saw this, too. His eyes, so long accustomed to the dark, made out a faint glow. He stopped short, pulling back on the cord.

"No! Wait!"

"Why? What is it, Hacon?"

To his vast relief, Nik heard the compliance in that query. The pull on the cord loosed. Vandy must have halted.

"I don't know yet. What do you see, Vandy—tell me!" That was an order.

"Shine—but just at one place," the boy reported. "It isn't a lure, I think. More like something big and tall just standing there waiting—" With each word a little of the confidence in his tone ebbed.

Then Nik heard a half whisper closer at hand, as if Vandy were shrinking back to him. "Not a story—"

"No, this is not a story, Vandy." He answered that straight.

"It—it wants us to come—so—so it can get us!" Vandy's whisper was a rapid slur of words.

And Nik felt that, also. Just as he had known earlier that sensation of a lurking watcher, so now he was caught—or struck—for that contact was as tangible in its way as a physical blow. Was it hatred, blind, unreasoning malice—that emotion beating at him? He was not sure of what had reached him like a spear point probing into shrinking flesh. He only knew that they were now fronting some danger quite removed from the animal furred hunters, from the Disians and their clawed hounds. This was greater, stronger, and more to be feared than all three of those native perils combined.

The blaster Vandy carried? The rayer in his own belt? Nik watched that gleam. Now he could see that it was as the boy reported—not a twinkling, dancing lure light but an upright narrow bar, unmoving as yet. Did it merely stand there to bar their way or was it gathering force for attack?

"It's—it's calling—!"

Vandy's body pressed against Nik. Perhaps that contact enabled him to feel it also. His arm went about the boy, holding him tight, while with the other hand he stripped off the second pair of goggles Vandy had hung about his neck. To put those on meant freeing the boy now threshing in Nik's grip, crying out with queer high-pitched ejaculations that sounded almost as if he were trying to mimic the whistles of the Disians.

171

"Must—go—" The words in Basic broke through those squeals. "It wants—"

Nik knew that already, the pull, the insistent, growing demand. He swung around, dragging the struggling Vandy with him so that his body was now a barrier for the boy. The goggles—he *had* to have sight again. He must get them on!

So, he took the chance of freeing his hold on Vandy. Struggling with fingers made awkward by haste, Nik slipped the straps over his head and adjusted the fastening. Vandy pushed against him, striking out madly with small fists to beat Nik out of his path.

Sight again. Nik blinked at that sudden transition and whirled about. Vandy was already well down the passage toward that pillar of cold light. *Cold* light? Nik wondered. Yet that was true. The cold radiating from that alien thing was eternal—alien as the rest of Dis, in spite of its weird life, was not. The hunters, the Disians, and their hounds were strange to off-world eyes, but this thing of the burrows did not share blood, bones, and flesh with any species remotely akin to life as Nik knew it.

Vandy was running, his head up, his eyes fastened on the thing. And once he reached it—!

The rayer! It might not act against that creature, but wearing goggles as he was, Vandy would be blinded by the ray, momentarily out of action. It was the only answer Nik could think of in those few seconds. He clawed his own goggles down as he fired.

Light flared above and ahead of Vandy as Nik had hoped. The boy cried out and reeled against the wall, his hands to his eyes. That swirling mist of light, strong as fire flames for Nik, must have been scorching for Vandy. Nik hurried forward, caught at the moaning boy, and pulled him back.

The attraction from the thing was shut off as if some knife had snipped a tug cord. They were free! Nik did not halt to put on his own goggles again. The light in the corridor made diamond-bright particles, giving him a start on the backward road. Vandy did not fight him now but lay, a heavy weight, on Nik's shoulder.

Then, it struck at him! Not with the drag to bring him back but with an invisible whip of cold rage so potent that Nik cried out as if a lash had truly been laid across his quivering skin. He had no experience with which to compare this torment, which was not of body at all. A curling thong of sensation first used to punish, then to wrap about him, to pull him in—

He fought that, holding Vandy's dead weight to him, fought the demand to turn, to march back, to deliver himself and the boy into deadly peril. Nik leaned, panting, against the wall. Vandy flung out an arm, his fist striking Nik's face, tangling in the dangling goggles. He was threshing for freedom again but more feebly. A last wriggle brought him out of Nik's weakening grasp—to fall to the pavement.

Nik turned slowly, his teeth set. How much of a charge did that rayer hold? Would it fail him this time? It took infinite effort to bring the weapon up and point it in the general direction of the sparkling mist that still marked his first shot.

Once more that burst of light, bearable, just bearable this time, to his ungoggled eyes. And once again the abrupt cessation of communication freed him. Vandy was on hands and knees, crawling, moaning. Nik caught him by the back of his tunic and pulled him to his feet. He could not carry the boy any farther, but perhaps he could support him along. Nik started them both at the best pace he could muster back toward the terminal chamber.

The second dose of raying must have reactivated some of the remaining sparks from the first, for the light behind them lingered, and Nik did not pause to reset his goggles. He waited for another sign that the thing would pressure them to its will. The blaster—could the blaster stop it more effectively? Vandy had a blaster—but even to stop to find it now might be greater risk than straightforward flight.

They reeled out of the passage into the terminal

chamber. Here the glow was only the faintest of glimmers. Nik allowed Vandy to slip to the floor again as he fumbled for the goggles. He was aware of an increasing cold, not in the atmosphere about him but within himself, as if in those two brushes with the alien's will he had been chilled, frozen. He could not still the shaking of his hands.

"Vandy." Nik leaned over the boy. "Come on—" He could not carry him. Vandy would have to help himself in part. Nik's hands brought him to his feet. But the boy's head hung down on his chest, and his body was racked with even greater shudders than shook Nik.

"This way—"

At least he kept on his feet and moving, as Nik steered him toward the passage that would retrace their journey. As they went, Vandy seemed to regain more conscious will, and the farther they moved from that weird battleground, the firmer his steps became. At last he looked up at Nik.

"What was—that?" His voice shook.

"I don't know."

"Will it—come after—us?"

"I don't know."

They were still in the lighted portion of the passage, but beyond was the dark strip in which the Disian ambush had been. Nik fingered the grip of the rayer. He had to save it for extreme emergencies.

"The blaster," he asked Vandy. "Where is it?"

"It's—it's not much use. I tried it after I used the other up on the worm things." Vandy pulled the off-world weapon from the front of his tunic. "It flickers some—"

Flickering, the sign of power exhaustion! They had not known how long the charges would last, and Vandy had exhausted one and nearly finished the other.

"But it still worked then?" Nik persisted.

"Yes."

A few moments of firing power must remain. That would have to be saved for most dire need—which left

174

the rayer, and how close that was to extinction Nik did not know.

They had reached the end of the lighted sector. Ahead was the dark and all it might contain. Nik looked back. Nothing behind, no glimmer of greater light, none of that menacing wave of broadcast fear. Perhaps whatever they had fronted had been bested by the second use of the ray or was confined for some reason to that special territory in the burrows.

"No!" Vandy's sudden cry startled Nik. The boy was staring ahead as if he sighted some trouble.

"What is it?"

"I don't want to go—not back there!"

"We have to!" Nik's patience and control had worn very thin. He wanted to get back to where he had left Leeds. That desire was an ache throughout his shaking body. Somehow that was a small island of security in this threatening underground world.

"I don't want to!" Vandy repeated, his voice rising. "It may be waiting there—to get us!"

"We left it behind," Nik pointed out, though he was dismayed by the tone of certainty in the boy's voice.

"It's—it's all wrong." Vandy spoke more quietly now. "It's not like all the others—the animals, the worms, the men you told me about. This—this can do things they can't!"

Like slide through solid rock walls? Nik forced his imagination under bonds. He could believe that, but allowing the idea to stop them on the mere suggestion that such action was possible was the rankest stupidity. They could not stay here forever, and he held to the thought of the Patrol's pursuit. To see even Commander i'Inad would give Nik a feeling of relief just now.

"We can't stay here, Vandy." Nik schooled his tone to an evenness and once more took firm hold of his patience. "And we know what is along this corridor. You don't—don't feel the thing ahead right now, do you?"

"No—" The admission was reluctant, but it was the one Nik wanted.

Vandy started on slowly, Nik's hand on his shoulder

175

to steady him. The dark swallowed them up. There was the sound of their own heavy breathing, the click of their boot plates on the rock under them, but Nik could hear nothing else. And there was no light ahead.

"Hurry!" His hold on Vandy tightened as he pushed the boy along.

"I can't!" Vandy's protest was half sob. Since their meeting with the thing, he had lost much of his self-assurance. "Hacon—the Patrol *is* coming?"

"Yes." Nik did not doubt that at all. He wanted to pick up Vandy and run—the feeling of urgency was a goading pain—but he knew he did not have the strength.

Then it came with a jolt—the throbbing whistle—and he could not tell if it broke from ahead or behind them. Nik only knew that the hunt was up, that he and Vandy were the prey.

"Hacon—" That was a gasped whisper.

There was no need to keep the truth from the boy.

"The Disians," Nik said. But had that call been behind or ahead? They could only keep on going. "Watch—for—any—lights—" he told Vandy between panting breaths. "Especially any that move—"

But the way before them remained safely dark. Nik tried to remember how long that dark sector had been. Surely soon they would sight the shrine of the next lighted portion near where the break in the wall gave on the outside.

"Hacon!"

Just as the whistle had been one alert, so this was another, this stroke of fear as sharp as physical pain. Nik paused to look back. No glimmer yet, but he was certain the thing had left its station and was on the prowl behind them.

"Keep going!" he ordered between set teeth. "Keep going!" They must make it back to Leeds.

Vandy, Nik thought, was crying silently now, but he was going on, and they had not yet been trapped in the net of the thing's compelling will. Each glance behind told him the enemy had not yet appeared, not in

176

person, but only in that black blanket of fear, which was one of its weapons.

The whistling began again, not in a single sharp throb but as a low, continuous bleat that filled the ears and became one with the blood of the listener. But, Nik realized, it did not become one with the fear projected by the thing. In fact, it warred with it so that the worst of that other depression lifted. Hunters who were natural enemies—who had *not* joined forces? Dared he hope that they might clash and so give their prey a fighting chance?

"Hacon, that noise—what's happening now?"

"That's the Disians' call. And I don't think the other thing is pleased—"

"Will they fight?"

"I don't know."

"There's a light—now!"

Vandy was right. There was a light ahead. But a second later Nik was filled with a vast relief. It was the end of the dark sector—not an attack signal. Once in the lighted passage, it was not too far back to Leeds.

"Just the passage light!" Relief made that almost a shout. "Keep going, Vandy, keep going!"

The whistling was louder, becoming a din, and under that lurked the fear. It was as if all the life that sulked in these burrows had been stirred into action. Could they, even if they reached Leeds, hold out against such a concentrated attack? But one thing at a time. Leeds knew more of Dis. He might have some answer to such danger. And there was the Patrol. Nik pinned his last hopes on the Patrol.

Vandy was weaving from side to side. Only Nik's grip kept him on his feet, but still he moved to that beacon of light. The pain had returned under Nik's ribs. It was sharp with every breath he drew. They must keep going—they must!

As suddenly as it had burst on their ears, the whistling stopped. Then the silence was worse than the din because Nik was sure it was prelude to action. And yet he did not know whether danger lay ahead or behind. He paused once again to look back and saw—

Lure lights! More than one, not only waving in the middle of the passage, but also from above and the sides, as if the Disian hounds clung to the walls and roof.

Nik and Vandy burst out of the dark and stumbled on. The boy looked back and gave a choked cry. Nik needed no alert against the nightmare boiling up there—the hounds coming at a scuttle.

"Vandy—give me the blaster!"

Nik jerked the weapon away from him. The charge might be almost gone, but perhaps enough remained to take care of the first attack wave. Only he must not use it until he was sure that no other party waited ahead to box them in.

Jointed clawed legs, round armored bodies—five—six—more coming through the dark. No sign of their Disian masters, if that was the relationship between the two so dissimilar species. They were slacking where the full light began. Nik thrust Vandy on with a powerful shove. The boy broke into a tottering run.

Nik was thankful that the creatures were not yet pressing the attack he feared. Then he wondered at that forebearance. Their rate of advance did not press the fugitives—why? He and Vandy were past the break in the wall. Just let them reach Leeds, and they would be able to hold off this pack with the second blaster the captain had.

Scuttle—click—but no more whistling.

"Keep going, Vandy!" Nik ordered. Then he saw their luck was beginning to fail; the creatures were drawing closer.

A throbbing whistle—

"Run, Vandy!" Nik got that out and swung around to face the pack. He pressed the firing button on the blaster.

A full beam answered! For an instant, he thought Vandy had been wrong about the weapon as that fan of

178

fire crisped the first wave of crawlers. Then a warning flicker rippled down the ray.

But the first burst had had its effect. The second group hesitated at the cindered bodies of their fellows. Nik backed away. Did he have charge enough left for a second shot? He must save that. And afterwards—the rayer?

Every stride he took was that much gained. Now the first of the pursuers had scrambled over the dead and were tentatively following. Just let them collect in a body once more, and perhaps he could kill enough to discourage the rest thoroughly. Such a thin hope—but about the only one Nik had left.

18

The blast had taught the Disian creatures a measure of caution. Thier advance slowed, and Nik hastened his own pace. He was sure Vandy was well ahead. And every moment he won, every stride he took, was a small victory.

But that breathing space was only temporary. Nik was warned by a new massing of the pursuers. And then he noted something that quickly revised his estimate of their intelligence. They were passing from one to another, over rounded shell backs, fragments of rock. Whether these were to be used as shields or weapons, Nik did not know, but he quickened his retreat.

A stone as big as his fist came at him, and he ducked. But his reactions were slow, and the missile grazed his head just above the goggle strap, so that he swayed back against the wall on his left. A blow on his shoulder before he had shaken free of the daze of that first hit numbed his left arm. He had not dropped the blaster, and for the second time he fired.

The beam was short, snapping out in a matter of seconds, but it curled up a row of the stone throwers and gave Nik time to lurch out of range. He had to make it—he had to!

At least he was coming out of the fog of pain that filled his head, and he had bought some more time. Time he could use—

"Hacon!"

The call sounded far away, but it pulled Nik together, and sent him scrambling ahead.

"Coming, Vandy." Had he answered that aloud?

An opening—the chamber where he had left Leeds! With a lung-emptying effort, Nik flung himself forward through that—and crashed into utter darkness.

"—easy—easy—easy—"

One word ringing in his aching head. What was easy? A faint stir of curiosity moved somewhere in the depths of Nik's darkened mind.

"—do as exactly as I say—say—say—" Echoes growing farther and farther away.

Do as who says—why? Again Nik was pushed into thought in spite of a desire not to be at all.

"—when they come, you will say this—this—this—"

Always the echo ringing in his ears as had the Disian whistles. Disian whistles! Memory awoke and prodded fiercely. Nik opened his eyes. There was a glimmer about him, a ghostly pallid counterfeit of true light. He was lying on his back, and his shoulder ached with a sullen, angry persistence.

"You understand it all now?" These were words with the crack of authority, a demand for obedience.

"Yes."

Vandy! There was no mistaking Vandy's voice. Vandy and—Leeds! Then they had reached the captain. But Leeds had to know about the hunters. They would be coming; they would erupt here! How long had he, Nik, been out? Another stone must have brought him down just as he came out of the passage—

"Captain?" That did not come out as a word. It was a rusty, croaking sound. Nik tired to turn his head, and a jab of pain followed, so intense as to make him sick. He retched dryly before he called again, "Captain?"

Movement through the gloom. Nik dared not move his head, but now he could see the shadow looming over him.

"Captain?" he asked for the third time.

"Right." But Leeds did not stoop. He remained a pillar hardly visible to Nik.

The dark! Nik made a vast effort and brought his hand up to his head. Before his fingers reached his eyes, he knew the answer. His goggles were gone. And he also guessed who wore them now. Just as that black and alien cloud of fear had closed on him back when he fronted the shining thing, so now he was uneasy. There was something wrong here—what?

"So, you're awake?" The cool voice rang in Nik's ears. In this half light, he could not read the expression on Leeds' face, but that tone— As if the captain were not standing there but had retreated to a far distance.

"The Disians—they are coming—" Nik gave his warning first. Again he tried to move, to see the opening through which they might rage. But the pain in his head and the answering agony in his shoulder kept him quiet.

"They haven't arrived yet." Again a certain cool disassociation with such concerns. "Vandy!" Leeds' head turned. "Get going!"

Going where, Nik wondered.

"Sorry." That was the captain. "You might have worked out—otherwise. Only I have to cut all losses now—"

Words that did not mean anything, or did they? Nik's wariness was acute. He made an effort, which left him sick and trembling, but he raised himself up on the elbow of his sound arm. Leeds stepped back.

"Where—are—you—going?" Nik got that out.

"To meet destiny—otherwise the Patrol."

"Back?"

"Back."

"Don't think I can—yet—"

"You won't be asked to try."

It took a long second for that to sink past the pain. Then Nik put a new fear into words.

"You mean—I stay here?"

Leeds was still retreating. "You stay. As you just said, you can't make it, and there's trouble coming. Hacon the hero is the proper rear guard, isn't he? Right in character to the end."

182

Nik still could not believe it. He pushed up to a sitting position and watched the dusky space about him twist sickeningly. One determination held through that whirling punishment. He would not beg.

Click of boots on rock—Leeds *was* going! He had Vandy back, he would make his deal with the Patrol—and he was leaving Nik as a rear guard or rather as an offering to whatever Disian pursuit existed. Yes, Nik was the price the captain was willing to pay for his own clear escape!

And what that sorted itself out in Nik's mind, he felt such rising anger as he had never known before in his short life. All the frustration and hatred stored up during the years in the Dipple were fuel for that rage. There had been nothing then he could do to fight back. But here and now he could do something, if it were only to draw after Leeds the very trouble he feared. Nik might not be able to walk, but he could crawl.

He hunched together, gathering strength. Goggles were gone again. Once he left this chamber, he would be plunged into the dark. His right hand moved along his belt—the rayer was gone. Well, he could not have expected Leeds to overlook that, could he? Nothing but his bare hands and the determination not to be counted out armed him now.

Nik made himself wait, hoping that he presented to Leeds, should the captain glance back, the picture of dejected submission to fate. It was still hard to think clearly. Only rage gave him the strength to make a move.

He could no longer hear the irregular tapping marking the captain's limping progress. And there had been no sound from Vandy at all. Nik raised his head. As far as he could see, he was alone. He could not get to his feet, but there were still his hands and knees—

Nik had to fight with every scrap of will within him to enter the dark beyond. No sound of footfalls ahead. But he was listening, too, for what might be behind.

The way might have been shorter for a man able to walk it, but to Nik, creeping along, it seemed endless.

He could put so little weight on his left arm that even his crawl was one-sided and slow.

Leeds and Vandy must have already reached the root room. Nik strove to hurry, but the greater effort brought back his giddiness. At least there was no whistling and none of that invisible menace cast by the other thing.

Nik tried to piece together what had happened in the immediate past. He had been running from the hounds and had just reached the lighted chamber when— Had one of the stones struck him or could Leeds have deliberately knocked him out?

Since their meeting at the island hill, Leeds had needed Nik—first to get the supplies, then to help him regain control of Vandy. Yes, Leeds had needed Nik. But now—did he need him any longer? Nik had been the one who had actually removed Vandy from the HS villa back on Korwar. Now Leeds could say that he had nothing to do with the kidnaping. He could return Vandy and make a much better bargain without Nik than he could if he tried to cover him with the same immunity. Leeds' present action was good sense if the captain wanted to make the best deal. Nik's sustaining anger grew with his realization of his own stupidity. Leeds had used him from the start—with bait he knew that Nik could not resist, a new face. And that, too, had all been part of the deception. There had been no new techniques used on him, no way to keep the operation intact for long. He was a temporary tool, to be used and discarded. Leeds had probably never even bought him into the Guild!

Nik crawled on. He wanted Leeds' throat between his two hands—that was the burning desire filling every part of him. But Leeds had Vandy, all ready to bargain with the Patrol. If only that bargain could be queered! To fail now would be worse for Leeds than any other hurt Nik could deal him.

What had been the bargain as Leeds had outlined it? To get a ship and free passage off Dis—then to release Vandy in a suit to be picked up by the Patrol. Nik licked his lips. Vandy released in a suit? Now he did not believe that either. Vandy could either be such a threat that his death *must* ensue, or he could be used again in some game for Leeds' advantage.

What had been Leeds' parting shot? Hacon the hero—Well, there was no future for Nik Kolherne, even if he were able to reach his own kind again and not be pulled down by some nightmare of these burrows. But he might accomplish something against Leeds—he had to! And perhaps he could make sure that the trickery that started in that Korwarian garden would finish here—that Vandy would not continue to be bait or loot or whatever Leeds wanted him to be.

The sickly light of the root chamber was ahead, and Nik remembered the drop from the crevice to the floor below. Would Leeds be lingering there or would he already have herded his captive on into the dark ways? Nik clung to the thin, very weak hope that the two were still in the root chamber. His chances of doing something in the passages beyond that point were close to the vanishing point. He wriggled forward to look into the room.

The light was greater because he had come out of the dark. Nik surveyed the scene with a deliberation he forced on himself. Leeds and Vandy were both here. The captain sat in much the same position as Nik had seen him—was it hours or days before?—examining the ties that held the splint on his wounded leg. His movements were slow, and he winced once. Nik was certain his injury was a drag.

Vandy was within arm's distance of his captor. He wore goggles, but his arms were tied behind him. Nik longed for one of the stones the hounds had thrown, though whether he could have used it to any purpose, he did not know. If he came into sight through the crevice, Leeds could pick him off before he reached the floor of the chamber.

Apparently the captain was not planning to move on at once. He opened a ration container and held it first to Vandy's mouth and then his own, so they shared the contents. Nik's empty stomach was a new source of pain as he watched.

"We shall give your friends"—Leeds' voice was still cool and light—"some more time. They were probably misled by the zeal of your late champion when he sent the tracer bag downstream. But you have your own way of contacting them, haven't you, Vandy? And I would suggest you use that gadget now."

Little of the boy's face could be seen below the masking goggles, but Nik noted the fining down of cheek and chin, the hollows beneath the grimy skin.

"You'll blast anybody that tries to come—"

Once more Nik heard that new maturity in Vandy's voice.

"On the contrary, my boy, I will welcome them with open arms. There is certainly no future here. And to return you to your anxious friends is a good way to get out, whole skin and free. You saw what I did to the man who brought you here in the first place."

"Hacon said—"

Leeds laughed. "My poor boy, please understand the simplest of truths—there is no Hacon, except in the wonderland of your own imagination. That port rat who pulled you into this mess is Nik Kolherne from the Dipple. He is not even a member of the Guild."

"You are." Vandy held to his point.

"I am Guild when it suits me to be and no time else! There's a big reward waiting for the man who returns Vandy i'Akrama—I want that and my ship. We'll make a bargain, and that is the last you'll see of me, I assure you. After all, Vandy, you have only to tell the truth. I *am* bringing you back; I *have* disposed of the man who stole you from Korwar. There isn't any scanner on this world or any other that wouldn't pass me clean on those two questions."

"What'll happen to Hacon—to him back there?" Vandy asked slowly.

"He'll stay and nurse a sore head until the Patrol wants to pick him up."

186

"But there were those other—other things. What if they find him first?"

Leeds shrugged. "All right, what if they do? He's no friend of yours. Now I'm telling you, boy, get out that fancy little com of yours and give it a tinkle. I heard that Commander i'Inad is with the Patrol—"

"Staven?" Vandy's head came up. "Staven's here? You'll have to untie me or I can't use the mike, you know."

"Yes. One hand, Vandy, just one hand. You're a slippery little fish, and you're not wriggling off until we are all safe and sound again. Turn around—"

The boy, on his knees, twisted around so Leeds could get at the ties on his wrists. Nik measured the distance he must drop, the space before the roots could give him limited cover. In his weak state, he had to have more time—

Vandy's free hand was at the breast of his tunic and came out with something cupped in the palm. He put it close to his lips and appeared to be breathing on it. Leeds watched him closely, the drawn blaster resting on his outthrust splinted leg.

Not a chance, thought Nik, not one little chance unless Leeds moved. In this light the captain's face was a blue mask of goggles and shadowed flesh. Blue—!

Nik stared, alerted now to the odd change taking place in the misty light of the chamber. It was blue! Not only that, but there was also a distinct chill in the air. He levered himself up so that he now crouched in the crevice. As yet, neither of those below apparently noticed the alteration in the atmosphere.

Movement! Nik wrenched his attention from Leeds and the boy to focus on movement among the entwined roots of the weird growth. Something alike in size and shape to those worm roots was edging out into the open. More than one—from other directions—!

"Any contact yet?" Leeds demanded.

Vandy was quiet. Then he stiffened. His hand dropped from his mouth, and his lips shaped a cry. Leeds followed the boy's horrified gaze and went into action.

Roots and that which moved from them crisped in an instant .

Only it was not the crawlers that were to be feared the most. Vandy was on his feet, backing away, not from Leeds or the remainder of the crawlers, but from a space below and to the left of Nik's perch. It was there, pulsating, growing, from nothingness into the totally alien shining thing.

Leeds fired again, this time directing his blaster at the growing core of light. And it absorbed the raw off-world energy of the weapon, seeming to suck the power away until Leeds looked down with terrified bewilderment at an empty tube. He began to back away as had Vandy.

The thing made no attack, no outward threat—it merely was. Nik wanted to draw back into the dark of the tunnel. Only one thing held him where he was— Vandy's face, upturned a little now to front the unknown.

Leeds had been right. Vandy was here only because of Nik Kolherne. And Nik Kolherne was finished any way you reckoned it. Better make it as good a finish as he had the chance to—

"Leeds!" Nik shouted. "The rayer—use the rayer!"

That blinding light had stopped the thing back in the tunnel and might be the only defense now.

Leeds' foot caught in a root tangle when he tried to move. Had Nik's call pierced through the wall of Vandy's terror? The boy flung himself on the captain, pawing at the other's belt as Leeds strove to throw him off. Something clattered, spun across the rock, and stopped at the very edge of the stream.

The pillar of light was growing closer to Nik. To reach that weapon, he would have to pass it, and every nerve shrank from any contact with that light. Vandy crept toward the rayer, but Leeds suddenly caught the boy by one foot and hurled him back and away. Had the captain gone mad?

Nik gathered his feet under him. He looked away determinedly from the pillar and concentrated on the rayer. Then he swung down from the crevice. The fringe of the light struck his left side. It was a cold so intense that he was numbed, and he tottered rather than leaped for the rayer.

A shout, and Leeds threw himself as if to intercept Nik. Sprawling forward, the younger man flung out his arm in a last desperate try, and his fingers touched the smooth metal. Somehow he turned over, aimed at the towering pillar of icy light, and pressed the button, praying that all its charge had not been exhausted.

There was a flash, blinding. And all the air was filled with a moaning—or did he feel rather than hear that? He saw Leeds crawling, his splinted leg trailing behind him, heading into the light.

"Leeds!" Had Nik shouted that warning aloud or was it swallowed up in the noise that was a part of the air, of him, of all this buried world?

At any rate, the captain did not heed. He crept on into the swirling light. And Nik knew that, wearing the goggles, the other had been blinded. Then he saw Vandy staggering forward, also being drawn on into the place where the pillar had stood.

Nik made a last effort, rolled his body across the boy's path, and threw up his good arm to prevent Vandy from merging with the chaos that had swallowed Leeds. He was still holding the weakly struggling boy, though he did not know it, when Vandy's call was answered.

The window was too high for Nik to see through, but outside was real sun. A bar of its light was warm across his hands and face. This was the first time he could remember rising from the bunk in the drab room and moving about. How long had he been here—and where was *here*?

Nik thought he *was* awake now, but for a long time he must have dreamed. Or could he call it dreaming just to remember every searing bit of his past, all the hurt from the moment he had been found in the wrecked ship up to that last sight of the burrows of Dis when he had concentrated on saving Vandy from the thing that walked there?

"Hacon!"

Nik continued to stare up at a cloud, which was the only moving thing the window allowed him to view. But he knew he heard that call in the here-and-now, not out of memory.

"There is no Hacon," he said harshly before he turned, his hand flying up in the old gesture to mask a face he had not dared to touch since his waking.

Vandy was there and a tall man in uniform—a man with Vandy's eyes.

"No need—" The tall man caught Nik's wrist and pulled his fingers down with a strength the other could not withstand. "Look!"

He was holding a mirror at the level of Nik's eyes, and the other could not defy that order.

"Not—not true!" Nik was shaken.

"What is not true? That you do not see correctly or that Leeds added another lie to all the rest?" asked the man with Vandy's eyes. "You see the truth—that face remains. Now, does the rest of it?"

"The rest of what?" Nik asked dazedly.

"Of Hacon?"

"But Hacon never existed—really."

"Did he not? My son created a man and then found him—"

Nik was still bewildered. But there was a smile on Vandy's face, and the man was continuing.

"My son dreamed of a hero, but he found the truth under the shell of that dream, masked by it. So, in creating a myth, he also brought forth new truth. We have in the past days learned what lay behind that mask, in the memory of Nik Kolherne—who is dead—"

So compelling was the emphasis in those words that Nik glanced at the bunk, half-expecting to see himself lying inertly there.

"For Hacon, Vandy and I have a certain responsibility. And we are deeply in his debt."

"But—I stole Vandy—took him to Dis—"

190

"And there you saved him, several times over, I would say. No—you are not Hacon, but neither are you any longer Nik Kolherne. Suppose you try being the man whose face you have earned. The price for a son comes high among our people. We will remember that when we meet with Hacon—"

Nik's hand went to his face again, but now he fingered smooth flesh. Only, more than his face had somehow been mended. He was not altogether sure he understood what the warlord meant, but he was willing to learn—to learn how to be someone who was not Hacon and a hero, or Nik Kolherne, who was nothing at all. There was no mask needed, and he had come out of the night indeed!

ABOUT THE AUTHOR

Andre Norton is an outstanding science fiction/fantasy writer who is best known for the strange, memorable, wholly believable worlds she creates.

She has received the coveted Gandalf and Balrog Awards, and her works have been translated throughout the world.

She lives in Florida.